Graham Canton's life has always revolved around his work as a Navy SEAL. When faulty Intel culminates in a mission going horribly wrong, he loses more than just part of his leg. He loses his identity. While Graham knows he should feel grateful he's returning home alive—after all, some on his team didn't—all he can think about is how life as he knows it is over. Then, living with his brother as he recovers, Graham meets Eban O'Gillie, and his life turns upside down all over again.

As a dominant great white shark shifter, Eban enjoys his role as head enforcer for his pod. His life at *World of Aquatica*, a marine park owned and operated mostly by aquatic shifters, couldn't be better. He loves helping his alpha and beta aid those under their care and figuring out their problems. Eban's first look at Graham is through a security camera, and his attraction is instantaneous. When he meets the human, all becomes clear. The injured veteran is his mate.

Can Eban show Graham that his worth is more than his ability as a SEAL while figuring out who's sending him hate-filled letters?

Chumming with a Great White
Copyright © 2020 Charlie Richards
ISBN: 978-1-4874-3060-3
Cover art by Angela Waters

Published by eXtasy Books Inc or
Devine Destinies, an imprint of eXtasy Books Inc

Look for us online at:
www.eXtasybooks.com or www.devinedestinies.com

Chumming with a Great White
Beneath Aquatica's Waves
Book Eight

By

Charlie Richards

DEDICATION

Grief changes us – the pain sculpts us into someone who under-
stands more deeply, hurts more often, appreciates more quickly,
cries more easily, hopes more desperately, loves more openly.
~Unknown

CHAPTER ONE

"Come live with me."

Arching his left eyebrow, Graham Canton barely managed to bite back his scathing, knee-jerk reaction of responding, "No way I want my baby brother takin' care of me."

The words would have revealed exactly how bitter Graham was about lying there in a hospital bed with his body beat to hell and half his right leg missing. He knew he should feel grateful to be alive. Except, with the loss of his limb, he could no longer work as a SEAL.

What the hell am I supposed to do with myself now?

Graham had joined up with the military the day after he'd turned eighteen. He'd worked damn hard to become part of the elite. His entire life had revolved around the missions that dropped him behind enemy lines, only relying on the faith in his brothers-in-arms, their skills, and their Intel.

Too bad the information on our last op was so faulty. Fucking pencil-pusher messing up —

"I mean it, Graham."

Grisham speaking again returned Graham's attention to his brother.

"Come live with me. I have room," Grisham urged again, concern gleaming in his hazel eyes. "There's a gym to do your physical therapy in the building, and—"

"Wait a minute," Graham cut in, holding up his right hand. At least it was no longer in a sling. "Since when does your building have a gym?" Then he forced his lips to curve into a wry smile. "And room? In your one-bedroom apartment? I

1

have no desire to sleep on your sofa, and I won't put you out of your bed."

To Graham's surprise, Grisham's cheeks took on a pinkish hue.

Huh.

"Uhhhh . . . I guess I forgot to tell you," Grisham muttered, rubbing the back of his neck in clear discomfort. "I moved."

"Moved?" Graham cocked his head. "When? Where?"

Grisham heaved a sigh as he settled in the chair beside the bed. "Eight months ago," he revealed. "And I never told you because first you were deployed, then you were in a coma, and then recovering." Grisham waved at Graham's prone form. "So, yeah. Been a little pre-occupied with makin' certain my only family survived."

Graham scoffed, unable to help himself. "How is this surviving?" he grumbled, anger causing his gut to churn. "I'm a fuckin' cripple."

"You're alive, damn it," Grisham shot back. "Stop bein' such a pussy." He narrowed his eyes as he leaned toward Graham. "So you lost your leg below the knee. You know there are people who run marathons on prosthetics?" The green in his hazel eyes began to dominate his irises, betraying his anger better than the harshness of his tone. "Where the fuck is the fire that used to drive you?"

"Overseas with the rest of my leg," Graham snapped back.

Grisham reached over and smacked Graham upside the head. "Snap out of it, bro." Without waiting for a response, he rose to his feet. "You're comin' home with me. I'll let the doc know so he can sign your discharge papers."

Gaping, Graham watched Grisham head toward the door. The back of his head stung a little, but it was the disbelief at his brother's actions that really kept him silent. As Grisham disappeared out the door, Graham realized he still didn't know where his brother lived.

"Bloody *World of Aquatica*," Graham grumbled as he eased his prosthesis onto the fabric-covered stump below his right leg. "And with a partner, no less. When the fuck was he going to tell me?"

Graham straightened on his bed before reaching for his cane. In truth, he understood how the news could have been missed. His brother was living with the same man who'd had him tied up in knots when they'd met briefly for coffee.

The day I nearly died from arsenic poisoning because some bigoted asshole police officer paid someone to off my brother.

With Graham ending up in the hospital for a couple of days, then returning to base for mandatory training before being shipped out on his last mission, a lot had fallen through the cracks. It wasn't as if he could call Grisham any time he wanted. Graham's mission had been a covert operation, so no outside communication.

"Enough," Graham grumbled. "Stop thinking about it."

The soft tap of someone knocking on his bedroom door caught Graham's attention. Even as he called, "Come in," he instinctively knew who it was. He'd only been living with his brother a week and a half, and he knew Cuzco—Grisham's partner—remained timid around him.

Of course, that could be because I snapped at him about not needing help the second day I was here.

Mentally wincing, Graham knew it hadn't been his finest moment. He'd only had the prosthesis for a week in the hospital before he'd been released to Grisham's care. He'd still been unsteady on it, and it took work to rise from the sofa. When Cuzco had seen him struggling, he'd hurried over to help.

Graham had pushed his hand away, grumbling, "I don't need help."

The look on Cuzco's face was just one more thing to haunt his dreams at night.

And my thoughts during the day. Just great.

"A-Are you ready to go?" Cuzco asked softly, twisting his hands before him. "The show starts in twenty minutes. I have the golf cart ready."

Nodding, Graham used his cane to push to his feet. "Yeah, Cuzco." He'd become steadier on his fake leg over the last couple of weeks, but there was no way he could hike all the way into the nearby marine park, and they both knew it. "Thanks for getting that for me."

"Of course." Cuzco's uncertain expression disappeared as his smile lit up his features. "You're family. We always help family."

Graham forced a return smile, even though he felt anything but happy. Still, he'd promised his brother that he would get out more. Fresh air would do him good, too.

"That's kind of you to say," Graham muttered as he followed Cuzco from his room, his gait a little slow, but at least he wasn't limping too badly. "I'm glad my brother has you."

Even though Graham still found it odd that Cuzco had caught Grisham's eye, let alone ended up so smitten, his words were true.

I'm happy my brother's life is on track. Now what am I supposed to do with mine?

Eban O'Gillie heard Ovram shout his name. Pushing to his feet, he rounded his desk and headed across the hall. He leaned against the open door and met the sea lion shifter's gaze.

"Yeah, Ov?" Eban asked, crossing his arms over his chest. "What's up?"

Ovram pointed at a security monitor. "I think we have an issue in the underwater aquarium."

Easing closer to the screen, Eban rested the knuckles of his left hand on the desk and took in the scene. The camera showed the wall of glass thirty feet away. Within the aquarium swam a vast array of fish, sharks, and other marine life.

Except, Eban knew that wouldn't be what Ovram was referring to. He swept his gaze over the large area full of milling humans who all appeared to be enraptured by the creatures beyond the glass. Well, all of them except one.

Near the far-left side of the viewing room stood a man leaning against the wall. He clutched a cane in his right hand, and he stared at the floor. Even through the camera, Eban spotted the slight sheen of sweat dotting the man's brows as well as the pallor of his skin.

Even obviously under the weather, this guy is handsome.

Huh. Weird thought, but damn.

Eban couldn't help but sweep his gaze over the guy a second time. He figured he was a little over six feet, and his shoulders were wide with a trim waist. The jeans he wore molded to his muscular thighs. Eban even found the day or so growth of dark hair on his cheeks and chin sexy.

"Should I send someone in security to see if he needs assistance?"

Ovram's question yanked Eban out of his admiration of the man. He opened his mouth as he straightened, intending to nod and order him to contact Dare—an enforcer for their pod who worked under him in security. Except, then Eban felt the great white shark he shared his spirit with rumble in the back of his mind, displaying displeasure at sending the unmated giant octopus shifter to see to the man.

Ooookay.

Still, Eban would heed his animal's desires. "I'll go myself," he told their marine park's tech guru. "I was about to head to lunch anyway. Maybe he's diabetic and needs food."

With the other shifter's jaw sagging, Eban hustled out of the office, then the security building. He strode swiftly through the park, his long legs closing the distance between him and the hot man on the monitor. Eban really hoped he arrived before someone else had offered assistance.

Eban didn't understand his desire, but he wasn't one to second-guess himself, and he never second-guessed his shark's instincts.

Heading down the ramp that led into the tunnel that led to the underwater viewing areas, Eban easily dodged between viewers. He arrived in the room he wanted in just over five minutes. In that time, the man hadn't moved.

Eban spotted a woman glancing the guy's way, her brows creased in an expression of concern. Catching her eye, he smiled at her and tapped the word *security* on his *World of Aquatica* shirt. She smiled and nodded, then returned her attention to the children with her.

Pausing a couple of feet from the man, Eban inhaled, intending to speak. The man's fragrance coated his nostrils, and he almost let the breath out on a moan. The human's earthy, masculine aroma was just about the best damn thing Eban had ever scented.

Mate!

Eban sucked in a sharp gasp as the realization burst through his brain like a wrecking ball. Arousal surged through his body, causing his blood to flow south. His fingers twitched with the need to touch the man before him.

Then Eban took in the state of his mate once more.

Right. Gotta help him first.

Clearing his throat, Eban mentally pulled his head out of his ass. "Excuse me, sir," he greeted softly. When that didn't get the man to stop focusing on the floor, Eban stepped even closer and touched his elbow. "Sir?"

Wish I knew his name.

The human jolted from Eban's touch. His head snapped up even as his balance wobbled. A grunt of pain escaped his lips, and he placed his free hand on the glass to steady himself.

"My apologies for startling you, handsome," Eban rumbled, gripping the man's upper arm in the hopes of offering support. "I'm Eban O'Gillie. I'm in security here. We thought you may need assistance."

The human's brown eyes narrowed a little as he looked up at him. "Why would I need assistance? I'm just standing here looking at the fish." As he spoke, he attempted to pull his arm from Eban's grip, but his unsteadiness made it difficult.

Even as Eban scented the lie, he eased his grip and lifted both hands in placation. He immediately wanted to touch again. Still, since his mate didn't seem amenable to that, yet, he didn't.

"I don't mean to presume," Eban began slowly. Knowing the man really did need assistance, and with his shifter instincts screaming at him to care for his mate, he tried again. Eban didn't want to embarrass the man, so he pitched his voice low as he spoke. "You're pale. Your skin is clammy, and you seem a little unsteady on your feet." Giving the man an encouraging smile, Eban added, "If you're diabetic and need some food, I'd be happy to escort you to one of our restaurants."

"I—"

The human took a clearly painful step, snapping his mouth shut. Wincing and keeping quite a bit of weight on his cane and the other hand on the glass wall, he growled under his breath. He paused, heaved a sigh, then focused on Eban.

"Yeah, I guess I do need a hand. Overdid it," he grumbled. "I just need to get to the cart outside." Frowning, he muttered, "Getting down that ramp was harder than I thought it'd be."

Eban nodded. While he didn't understand what caused his mate's pain, it was obvious he was recovering from something. "I'd be happy to help." Slotting up close to the man, Eban wrapped his arm around his waist. His palm warmed where he rested it on the man's hip, feeling hard muscle beneath the jeans. "Lean on me, and we'll get you somewhere to get off what ails you."

"Thanks," the man mumbled, leaning against him and allowing him to help.

As they moved slowly up the ramp, Eban struggled with what to say. He'd never been the most sociable guy, but this was his mate. He needed to know at least something about him so he could find him again.

"I'm Eban," he repeated. "What's your name?"

"Graham," the human replied.

Eban nodded. "So, Graham, are you here with a group? Spouse? Family? Friends?" Realizing he sounded like he was putting the man through an inquisition, he quickly added, "What brought you to *World of Aquatica* today?"

To Eban's relief, Graham answered his awkward questions.

"Came with Cuzco to see the tiger shark show." Graham hissed, pausing for a second. Beads of sweat popped out on his forehead. "He works here. You know him?"

"Yeah, I know Cuzco," Eban replied, nodding. The other shifter shared his spirit with a small coconut octopus. "I believe he just went on shift."

That would explain why Graham was on his own.

Graham nodded. "Yeah."

They started moving again, and Eban saw the exit coming into view. His heartbeat sped up as he realized his time with his mate was coming to an end, and he still knew nothing about him.

"How do you know Cuzco?" Eban asked. At least he would have someone to ask about his mate after he left.

"He's my brother's partner. They're letting me crash in their spare bedroom for a while."

Upon hearing that, it was Eban's turn to pause.

That drew Graham's attention, and the man peered up at him. Something in Eban's expression must have concerned

Graham, for he narrowed his eyes. "Don't tell me you're big-oted."

"What?" *Get it together, idiot!* "No. No, not at all." Eban winked at Graham. "You did hear me call you handsome ear-lier, right?"

"Uhhh . . ."

Eban chuckled as he grinned down at him. Who he held in his arms finally clicked into place. His struggle with walking made sense now.

"You're Graham Canton, Grisham's brother." Upon seeing the wary nod, Eban squeezed Graham's hip and started them moving again. "Thank you for your service," Eban stated, holding his mate close as he referred to his time in the mili-tary.

And now he's home, here, and I'm gonna find a way to take care of him.

Except, even as Graham continued to move, his entire frame tensed in Eban's arms. "How do you know about that?"

"I'm head of security," Eban revealed, trying to soothe him. At the same time, he smiled at Graham and gave a half-shrug. "I know just about everything that goes on around here."

CHAPTER TWO

Graham nodded slowly, forcing the tension to leave his body. Leaning against the larger man felt a little too good. At least the pain throbbing up the stump of his right leg kept him from getting a boner.

"Makes sense," Graham murmured as Eban guided them outside. "There's my cart." He used his chin to point to the left and the cart waiting there.

Eban headed them that way.

To Graham's surprise, Eban urged him into the passenger seat. "Wait." Gripping one of the bars that supported the cart's roof, he stood on his left foot. "What are you doing?"

"Get in, Graham," Eban told him. "I'm taking you home."

Graham frowned as Eban rounded the front of the vehicle. "I can drive myself."

"I'm sure you can," Eban responded even as he slipped into the driver's seat. He held out his hand and wiggled his fingers. "Keys."

"Then—"

"Why am I doing this?" Eban cut in, finishing Graham's question for him. After giving him a lascivious once-over, he stated, "To spend more time with you, handsome, and perhaps convince you to have dinner with me."

Graham knew there was no way to misinterpret Eban's look, but he still didn't understand it. As he dug the cart's key out of his pocket, he muttered, "Dinner?"

"Yep." Eban took the key. "Hop in, Graham."

With a sigh of relief, Graham settled on the seat and placed his cane between his legs.

"Besides," Eban continued as he started the cart and began driving. "Driving with your left foot is awkward as hell."

Tensing, Graham frowned at Eban. "What the hell is that supposed to mean?"

Eban winced, glancing his way before refocusing on his driving. "I know what your injuries are, Graham."

Graham growled softly. "Why were you told?"

Why would my brother do that?

"Does everyone here know?"

"No," Eban stated with a sharp shake of his head. "Only a select few. Those in the inner circle. Everyone else just knows you're living here." Clicking his tongue, he muttered, "Probably too soon to talk about that." Eban rubbed his palm over his chin. "At least your brother and Cuzco can help when explanation time comes."

Graham cocked his head. "What are you talking about?"

Eban reached over and settled his palm on Graham's left thigh. Massaging lightly, he stated, "In private, handsome. Not in the park. Too many ears here."

Glancing from where Eban brazenly squeezed his thigh to the people they passed, Graham cleared his throat. Even as unease slithered through him upon hearing the bigger man's confusing words, he felt arousal burn through his veins. Eban's touch caused butterflies to bounce around in his belly, confusing the hell out of him.

Sure, Graham could admit Eban was a good looking man, but he was in no position to pursue anything . . . with anyone. His body ached most days, and his healing scars were a roadmap telling of his battles. He didn't even like looking at himself in the mirror.

"I sure ain't handsome," Graham muttered.

And that probably isn't what I should be focusing on.

Eban hummed. "I disagree."

Graham wondered at what kind of discussion couldn't be

done around the crowds. Had his brother been roped into an operation doing something illegal because he was in love with Cuzco?

"I can feel the tension in your thigh, Graham," Eban commented quietly. "Please try to relax. Whatever you're thinking . . . no."

"And what do you think I'm thinking?"

Graham forced his body to relax. He turned his head and stared at Eban's profile, taking in the man's brown eyes, hard mouth, and broad body. His frame was that of a warrior, all hard muscles and strong lines.

Eban glanced Graham's way, and his intense dark eyes seemed to soften for an instant as he looked at him. "For some reason, everyone's first guess is something illegal." His firm lips curved into a small smile. "There's nothing illegal going on here." Then Eban hummed, and he lifted his hand off Graham's thigh and waggled it in a *so-so* gesture before returning it to Graham's leg. "Okay. I admit, there's a few things that occasionally skirt the law, but once we've finished explanations, you'll understand why."

"And why would you tell me?" Graham asked uneasily. "And you just met me. Why does your hand on my thigh feel hella-possessive?"

And hella-good.

Graham didn't tell him that, though.

"Since your brother is already part of our culture, because you're already living in the community, and due to who you are to me, we'll tell you."

"Well, that was about as clear as mud," Graham grumbled.

"And, yeah, I'm gonna be hella-possessive," Eban added with a squeeze to his leg. "Because you're important to me."

"You don't even know me," Graham pointed out. His pulse spiked a little as discomfort flooded him. He shifted restlessly in his seat. "Chemistry aside, maybe we won't like each other."

Eban growled softly under his breath as he slid his palm between Graham's thighs and massaged along his jeans's inseam. "Glad you mentioned that chemistry, handsome. Should we skip dinner and get straight to the fucking?"

Graham gasped as his dick thickened behind his fly. "Damn. You're forward."

He couldn't believe the way his cock twitched just from Eban's light stimulation. Was it just because it had been so very long since he'd felt the touch of another? Gritting his teeth against his urge to shift in his seat so he could get Eban's hand a little bit higher, he tried to get his brain back online.

"I *am* forward," Eban remarked, moving his hand back to the top of Graham's thigh. "Especially when I see something I want."

Scoffing, Graham shook his head. His mind reeled. He couldn't figure out what Eban's game was.

Having left the park behind and almost reaching the apartment and condominium community, Graham shifted restlessly in his seat. Indecision filled him. He needed advice.

Graham just managed to keep from rolling his eyes. "I'm calling Grish," he claimed, pulling out his phone.

For a second, Graham wondered if Eban would try to stop him, but he just gave him a rakish grin and stated, "Tell him you're my mate, and we'll need to do explanations when he gets home from work."

"Uhhhh . . . what the hell does that mean?"

Eban chuckled. "Grish will understand, and when he gets home, we'll tell you." Releasing Graham's thigh, he pulled out his own phone. "Guess I better make a few calls, too."

Graham called Grisham's number as Eban made a call of his own. By the time his brother picked up, Eban had stopped and shut off the cart.

"Hey, Graham," Grisham greeted. "What'd you think of the show?"

Suddenly, watching the tiger shark show seemed so far in the past, Graham barely remembered that was why he'd gone to the park with Cuzco to begin with. "Uh, it was good. Interesting." He chuckled as he recalled the large shark leaping from the water to crunch massive hunks of meat. "Odd to see a shark do that."

"Cuzco tells me it's a park favorite," Grisham told him, a smile in his tone as he spoke of his man. "He said you stayed to explore the park. Find anything interesting?"

"Found some*one* interesting," Graham replied, glancing toward Eban, who winked at him.

"Some*one*?" Grisham hummed. "Really? Tell me. Anyone I know?"

"Do you know Eban O'Gillie?"

"I do." Grisham suddenly sounded concerned. "Stand-up guy. Good to have at your back. How'd you meet him?"

"I'll tell you about that later," Graham countered. "He drove me back to your place. Says I'm his mate, and that nothing illegal is going on here. What's he mean by explanations tonight after you get home?"

"Oh, damn," Grisham murmured. "His mate? He said that?"

"Told me to tell you that, yeah." Graham scowled upon hearing the amazement in his brother's voice. "What's it mean?"

"Uh, well, nothing bad," Grisham quickly told him. "But he's right. Explanations tonight in person." Then a husky chuckle sounded through the line. "Why don't you let him distract you from waiting this afternoon by having a fuckfest?"

Graham's jaw sagged open for an instant. Snapping it closed, he turned his attention to Eban. The man was staring right back at him, his brown eyes smoldering, the phone held to his ear apparently forgotten. A fresh burst of arousal heated

Graham from the inside out. He couldn't ever remember being the recipient of such a look.

"Yes, Alpha," Eban stated.

Okay. Not forgotten.

"Ask Grisham what time he should be home," Eban instructed, pointing at the phone Graham continued to hold.

Graham had to clear his throat in order to ask, "Eban wants to know when you're supposed to be home tonight."

To Graham's surprise, Grisham barked a laugh. "Guess he heard my comment about fucking. My shift ends at six, but you know if I get called to a scene, it could be later."

"Tell him to text me when he gets off shift," Eban instructed, having obviously heard.

Damn, the man must have good ears.

Graham relayed Eban's order.

"Will do," Grisham replied. "So, first, no, nothing illegal. Whatever you're thinking is gonna be way off base. Second, take my advice and allow Eban to relax you all afternoon. You won't regret it." Before Graham could think up a response, Grisham continued, "Oh, and third, you won't need to use rubbers with him."

"What?" Graham couldn't think of anything else to say.

Talking about sex with Grisham was uncomfortable enough. Talking about it with Eban listening to every word just made it so much worse.

"Brother." Grisham's tone turned serious. "Just trust me."

"I trust you."

"Got another call coming in," Grisham told him. "I'll see you tonight."

Then Grisham disconnected, leaving Graham with an obviously horny and dominant man and more than a little confusion.

Eban knew Graham was beyond confused and more than a

little leery. His mate would understand in time. At least Grisham had given him a good endorsement.

Nice of him.

"Let's go inside, Graham," Eban urged. "Get that prosthesis off and you more comfortable."

Alone time with my mate. Gods, I've been waiting for him for so long.

Alpha Kaiser had encouraged Eban to take the afternoon off if he had the opportunity to spend it with Graham. Even just sitting and talking would help strengthen their bond.

"Besides," his alpha had commented with a chuckle. "You won't be able to concentrate on your work now anyway."

"Okay," Graham replied simply. Except, when Graham tried to stand, he groaned and sat back down. "Damn."

Eban rushed around the cart and stopped in front of him. Resting his hands on Graham's upper arms, he offered, "Do you want me to carry you?"

Scoffing, Graham smirked up at him. "Seriously? I know you're a big guy and all, but no way can you carry me."

With a wink, Eban murmured, "Is that a challenge?"

Graham shook his head. "Didn't mean it like that."

"That's okay." Eban slid his hands up to cradle Graham's jaws. "Is it a pride thing? Or do you really just not trust me to carry you?"

Eban watched as Graham's lips parted. His mate's tongue slipped out and slid over his lower lip. Swallowing hard, he longed to follow that same path with his own tongue.

So I think I will.

Dipping his head, Eban flicked out his tongue and licked Graham's lower lip. His mate's masculine flavor burst across his taste buds, setting his blood on fire. Eban needed more, so he sealed his lips over Graham's and pushed his tongue into his human's mouth.

To Eban's pleasure, Graham welcomed him. His tongue glided against his own as he began to slowly map his mate's mouth. He teased and tasted, reveling in the sensual flavor of his forever love.

Eban heard a wolf-whistle and felt Graham startle. Easing the kiss to an end, he smiled at his mate before turning his head and spotting Pisces, a dolphin shifter. The other man winked and gave Eban two thumbs up before heading into another building.

"Guess we should move this inside," Eban rumbled softly. "If you give me your keys, I can run inside and get your crutches. You can take off your prosthesis here instead."

Graham hesitated an instant, then nodded his head. "Okay." After digging out his keys, he handed them over. "I'm assuming you know which one?"

Eban nodded. "Yeah. We moved them to the third floor when Grisham and Cuzco told us they needed a second bedroom."

"What?" Graham's eyes widened, and his scent betrayed his surprise. "They moved for me?"

Oops.

Rubbing the backs of his fingertips along Graham's stubble, Eban told him, "This is community housing, paid for by the marine park. It was an easy move." He pecked his lips to Graham's again, then eased away a step. "I'll be right back."

Eban strode swiftly into the condominium building. Skipping the elevator, he headed to the stairs and took them two at a time until he reached the third floor. He turned left and crossed to the door he needed.

Once inside the two-bedroom, two-bath space, Eban took a discreet sniff. He easily figured out which room was his mate's and headed inside. Spotting the crutches leaning against the wall near the nightstand, Eban grabbed it, all the while wondering if he would be able to put that bed to good use very soon.

As Eban headed back outside, he fought back a grin. He'd scented the embarrassment mixed with arousal wafting from his human when Grisham had suggested a fuck-fest. Eban had become hard as a rock in seconds.

Wonder if I can convince him.

Returning to the front, Eban saw Graham hadn't removed his prosthesis, yet. He sat in the cart, his hands gripping the head of his cane, and he stared at the ground. It was the same brooding expression Graham had sported when he'd first spied him on the security screen.

"Here's these," Eban stated, announcing himself and holding out the needed items. "Can I take your cane?"

Graham nodded, swapping items with him. Then he levered to one foot and his crutches. Without a word, Graham started toward the door.

Eban opened it for him, then crossed the lobby with him.

Pausing, Graham pointed at the wall of mailboxes. "Can you snag my mail for me, please?"

"Sure can." Eban did as Graham requested as his mate hit the button for the elevator. Then he joined him as Graham held the door open for him. "Want me to flip through these for you?"

While Eban figured it was nosy of him, he wanted to learn about Graham any way he could.

Graham shrugged. "Go for it." Then he hit the button for his floor.

Most of the letters were addressed to Cuzco and Grisham. He spotted one to Graham that appeared to be from the military. "Should I open it?" he asked as he followed Graham out of the elevator.

Graham shook his head. "Naw. Probably more medical crap. I'll read it later."

Eban nodded as he finished flipping through the rest of the pieces. "Huh. This one doesn't have a return address."

Seeing Graham freeze beside him, Eban eyed his mate. His human's face paled a little as a growl rumbled from him. "Just toss it," he ordered.

18

"You know who it's from?" Eban asked curiously as he followed Graham into the condo he shared with his family.

Hopefully, he'll be sharing one with me soon.

"No," Graham replied while Eban closed the door behind them. "Just some hateful shit. Not worth reading, anymore."

"Hateful shit." Eban couldn't resist tossing the rest of the mail onto the front hall table and tearing it open.

"Eban, really."

Graham began reaching for the letter, but Eban took a step away from him as his heartrate spiked at what he was reading. Without even finishing it, he met his mate's gaze. He held up the letter.

"How often do you receive this kind of shit?"

His mate was being targeted.

CHAPTER THREE

K eeping the prosthesis off the floor, Graham hobbled to the sofa. He heaved a sigh as he settled on it. After placing the crutches aside, he began folding up the bottom of his boot-cut jeans.

"Graham?" Eban settled beside him. "Please talk to me."

"What's to say?" Graham replied, annoyance filling him. "I get a letter maybe once a week, and after the third one, I stopped reading them."

They'd all said pretty much the same thing just in a variety of ways. He didn't deserve to live. He shouldn't have been the one to come back. He should have lost more than his leg. Don't bother building a new life, because he wouldn't be around long enough to enjoy it.

Eban growled. "Someone is threatening you, my mate," he stated, as if Graham didn't already know that. "I just found you after two centuries of searching. No way am I letting some stalker asshole take you from me now."

Graham paused where he'd finally finished rolling his jeans up enough to reach where his prosthesis attached just below his knee. "I'm sorry. What?"

Frowning at him, Eban muttered, "What? You're my mate, goddammit, and my pod protects what's ours." Without further explanation, the big man rose back to his feet and pulled out his phone. Lifting it to his ear, Eban glared in the general direction of the dining room. "Alpha Kaiser, my mate has a stalker."

Returning his focus back to removing his fake leg, Graham

listened with half an ear to Eban's side of the conversation.

"I'll ask him." Eban touched Graham's shoulder, drawing his attention. "Have you reported this to your brother to open a file?"

Shaking his head, Graham grimaced upon seeing the thoughtful expression on Eban's face.

"Okay, good." Eban grunted before winking at Graham, his tone turning a little feral. "We'll handle this in-house then."

Graham sighed deeply as he finally removed his leg. After setting it aside, he took off the cap that supposedly protected his still-healing stump. He figured if Eban was serious about being interested in him, he should see the damage sooner rather than later.

Grimacing, he peered at the red and inflamed flesh. He had definitely been walking around the marine park far longer than he should have. Over three hours on his feet was a good hour and a half too long.

His doctors had warned him not to push too hard, or he would set himself back.

"Damn, handsome," Eban's soft voice cut into his musings. "Do you have some lotion or something to massage into your skin?"

Looking up, Graham took in Eban's expression. While his eyes held a wealth of concern, he didn't spot any pity or disgust.

"Why do you insist on calling me handsome?" Graham asked curiously. He waved at his leg. "Clearly I'm not, and these aren't my only scars."

Eban scoffed softly, shaking his head. "Scars don't make someone ugly, Graham." He shrugged. "And I have plenty of my own." As if to hit his point home, he grabbed the bottom of his polo and yanked it over his head. "See."

Graham felt his eyes widen as he took in Eban's expansive

torso. While he noticed the extensive scarring covering his right shoulder and upper pectoral, he couldn't help feeling a burst of arousal for a whole different reason. Eban's smooth, toned flesh and ripped eight-pack begged to be worshiped with his hands, lips, and tongue. His mouth watered, and his fingers twitched as blood filled his prick to half-mast.

Chuckling softly, Eban turned a little, revealing the massive network of scarring over his upper arm and halfway down his back.

"Damn," Graham whispered. "How'd that happen?" He squinted as he leaned forward. "It looks like a massive bite mark."

"It is," Eban confirmed. "Got into a fight with a great white." He waved his hand dismissively. "But that's my point, right?" Lowering to his knees, Eban rested his hands on Graham's knees. "I have plenty of scars, too, but I can smell your arousal. You're attracted to me anyway."

"Smell?" Graham whispered. "You say the weirdest shit sometimes."

Eban shrugged one massive shoulder. "I'll explain this evening. All I ask is that you remember these few things." He began rubbing over Graham's knees as he continued, "You are always safe with me, no matter what. Your brother is part of our family, and so are you. This marine park is a safe place."

While Graham didn't understand why assuring him of his safety was the important thing, he still nodded. His attention was too riveted on the fact that Eban was sliding his hands upward . . . toward his groin. His gut clenched, and he shifted restlessly.

Except, that caused the edge of his stump to slide along the sofa. Discomfort course through his angry flesh. He grimaced and rested his hands on Eban's.

"You okay?" Eban asked with concern. Then he glanced at

his leg. "Of course you're not. So, about that cream?"

Graham nodded. "In my bathroom. Second shelf on the left. It's in a little tub."

Eban nodded as he rose to his feet. Then, to Graham's surprise, he bent and pecked a kiss to his lips before heading away. "Be right back."

Sighing deeply, Graham relaxed on the sofa. His brain whirled with all the weird shit Eban had been spouting for the last hour. He didn't understand anything that seemed to be going on, but his brother had assured him that Eban was a stand-up guy and on the up and up.

Just what the fuck is going on here?

Except, as Graham watched Eban return with the cream, he wondered why he cared when he had a sexy-as-fuck man making a blatant advance.

If we fuck, am I thinking with my dick?

Maybe that wouldn't be such a bad thing. He hadn't gotten laid in over a year.

When Graham reached for the tub of cream, Eban shook his head. He knelt before him again. Then he proceeded to slather the cream on his stump, never once flinching or shying away as he gently massaged Graham's ruined flesh.

For some reason, that made Graham's dick even harder.

Yeah. Time to trust my brother and think with my dick.

Huh. That's a weird thought.

Eban watched as Graham relaxed under his attentions. For an instant, he wasn't certain his mate would allow him to care for him. His leg had been tense under his fingers, the thigh muscles twitching beneath their jeans covering.

After a few minutes of Eban lightly rubbing the cream into each scar, crevice, and puffy inch of skin, Graham had calmed. The acrid scent of tension and unease disappeared. In another moment, it was replaced by the most potent and heady aroma.

Oh, my mate is aroused.

The scent caused a predictable reaction on Eban's body. His own cock twitched behind the fly of his khaki shorts. He silently cursed the briefs he wore, only because he'd been on duty.

Once Eban was certain he'd coated every bit of Graham's stump and irritated flesh, he grabbed his polo shirt from the floor and used it to wipe his fingers. "How's that feel, Graham?"

Graham's deep brown eyes narrowed, and he peered at him with a heavy-lidded gaze. "My leg feels good, thanks." Even as his lips twitched in a semblance of a pained smile, the smell of his arousal never waned. "Never thought about how someone else, a prospective lover, would view my missing limb." As Graham held Eban's gaze, he admitted, "Finding someone wasn't even a blip on my radar."

"It wasn't for me, either, handsome," Eban told him softly. "A shifter never knows when their fated mate will appear, but we're always grateful for when it happens."

Upon seeing Graham's eyes narrow and some of his relaxed expression eased, Eban winced. "Damn. Being aroused around you really loosens my tongue."

Graham sighed deeply. "Damn." He tipped his head back a second and closed his eyes, then counted to three under his breath. Finally, Graham opened his eyes and stared straight at Eban. "I heard you use the term Alpha. You're a paranormal," he whispered. "Is Cuzco one, too?"

Eban's jaw sagged open. His eyes widened, and his breath caught in his chest. For a second, he felt as if his lungs forgot how to work.

How the fuck does he know about us?

Lifting a hand in placation, Graham murmured, "Relax. I'll never tell a soul. You have my word."

"Yes, I am a type of paranormal," Eban confirmed. "How

do you know about us?"

Humming quietly, Eban told him, "One of the men in my old unit is a vampire. We all knew, and a few of us occasionally offered him our blood when we were deep in-country and he couldn't find a source." He shrugged once, his expression turning sad and the scent of his arousal waning. "His abilities are the reason I'm here, but we had to fudge the reports. We all should have died, but he saved me and one other guy."

"Damn," Eban murmured, his mind reeling. "What's his name? Does he have a coven?"

Graham cocked his head. "No coven." His cheeks actually took on a pinkish hue. "He said his master kicked him out and named him rogue. Since he had nowhere to go, he joined the military."

"Well, if he wants a place to go now, he'll have one," Eban declared, squeezing Graham's thighs. "Anyone who saves the life of my mate is welcome here."

Nodding, Graham murmured, "I'll send Price an email asking him to visit." He shrugged. "I have no idea if he'd be interested in joining whatever your group is." Cocking his head, Graham pointed out, "But you called yourself a shifter. Does that mean you're a group of wolves or something?"

"Or something," Eban confirmed, then twitched the corner of his lips into a wry smile. "Guess sex is off the menu for a while if you're already aware of paranormals and you're asking questions."

Graham groaned. "I want to say yes and ask a shit-ton of questions, but now not needing a condom makes sense, and I so fucking want your dick in my ass." Reaching down, he rubbed at his swollen groin, yanking a moan from Eban's throat. "Just tell me one thing."

"Anything," Eban murmured, his focus riveted to where Graham touched himself. He wanted to swat his mate's hand away from there and replace it with his own. He wanted to open those jeans and —

"What's it mean when you say I'm your mate?"

Eban yanked his brain out of the gutter. He jerked his focus back to Graham's face. The human he soon hoped to make his lover stared at him intently. His eyes were narrowed, and his face remained a bit flushed, betraying his arousal as much as his scent.

"Did Price tell you what a beloved is?" Eban asked.

Graham shook his head.

Struggling with where to start, Eban decided to jump right in the middle. "A fated mate to a shifter is the one person they can bond with, twine their lives with, and spend the rest of their days caring for, pleasing, and doing everything they can to keep them happy and healthy." He hesitated for an instant, then added, "You asked if Cuzco was a paranormal. The answer is yes. He's a shifter, too, and your brother is his mate. They've bonded, have twined their life-threads, and will remain devoted to each other for the next several hundred years."

Blowing out a breath through pursed lips, Graham held Eban's gaze. "Sooooo . . . you want me for your mate. Your spouse."

Since it wasn't a question, Eban didn't comment with more than a nod.

"How do you decide on a mate?" Graham asked curiously. "And how does one bond?"

Eban smiled, appreciating that Graham wasn't freaking out on him. "Although we would have been attracted to each other regardless, Fate chooses our ideal mate." With a lascivious wink, he added, "Fate just happens to ramp up our desire when we meet him or her." Sliding his hands up Graham's thighs, Eban dug his fingertips into the crease of his groin. "And a paranormal's mate's libido will increase, urging him or her to accept his soul's other half."

Clearing his throat before swallowing hard enough to cause his Adam's apple to bob, Graham mumbled, "Okay." He rested his hands on Eban's wrists and held on tightly. "And bonding?"

"A paranormal male will make love to his mate, giving him or her as much pleasure as possible." Eban couldn't control how his voice grew husky with his desire as he envisioned doing just that. "Then, I will spill in you and sink my teeth into your neck." Reaching up, Eban touched Graham's neck. "You will orgasm from it . . . every time."

"Huh," Graham murmured, tipping his head to the side, offering him more room. "That doesn't sound too bad. Haven't had an orgasm in a long damn time."

Growling low in his throat, Eban whispered, "How many orgasms must I promise you in order to convince you to come to bed with me?"

Graham chuckled huskily, a small smile twitching the corners of his lips. "I'm pretty sure this doesn't have anything to do with orgasms. I—"

The sound of someone knocking on the door drew Eban's attention. Gritting his teeth, he drew away from his mate. "Just a second."

Eban rose to his feet and crossed to the door. He inhaled deeply and recognized the scent of Westram, one of their enforcers. Opening the door, he arched a brow in silent question.

"Alpha Kaiser asked me to swing by," Westram told him, rubbing the back of his neck. "Something about a letter?"

Knowing how distracted Westram had become over the last couple of weeks, Eban cut the longnosed saw-shark shifter some slack. The poor man was still trying to convince Noah—a friend of Alpha Kaiser's mate, Arthur—that his interest was sincere. One wrong comment, coupled with Dare hooking up with Noah's friend, Jacob, along with an unhealthy past relationship, and Westram was having a damn difficult time wooing his mate.

"Yeah. Let me get it." Eban turned back and spotted how Graham had pulled a throw blanket that had been on the back of the sofa over his lap. While he planned to ask about that, he crossed to the coffee table where he'd left the letter. "Do you have a bag, Westram?"

After seeing his enforcer shake his head, Eban changed direction and crossed to the kitchen. "Where are your plastic bags, Graham?" he called as he started to open cupboard doors.

"I think the kind you're looking for are in the narrow cupboard to the left of the refrigerator."

Eban opened the indicated cupboard and spotted the boxes stacked on top of each other. After a quick read-through of the labels, he pulled out a carton holding quart-sized baggies. He pulled one out, then returned the box and closed the door.

Placing the letter and envelope in the bag, then sealing it, Eban returned to Westram who was waiting beside the front door. "Take this to Emmanuel," he ordered. "Ask him to lift for prints. Mine will be on there, but he has those on file."

Westram's eyes widened a little. "Yes, Enforcer." Then the other man left.

Turning back to Graham after locking the door, Eban took in his mate's narrowed eyes.

"We have a lot to discuss," Graham commented, cocking his head. "Don't we?"

Eban nodded. "Yeah."

Graham shoved off the blanket, then grabbed for his crutches. "After you fuck me." Once he'd gained his feet, he warned, "Better not bond us, yet, though. Don't want your life in jeopardy in case that crazy stalker follows through on their threats."

Growling low in his throat, Eban stalked toward Graham. "Not a fucking chance." He wrapped his arms around his soon-to-be lover and held him close. "I will bond us and keep you safe for all time."

Snorting softly, Graham pointed out, "I was a Navy SEAL, Eban. I'm pretty good at taking care of myself."

"And after we bond, your healing will speed up," Eban pointed out, indicating his leg. "And you will grow stronger, allowing you to adjust more swiftly."

Graham hesitated, and Eban counted that as a win. Ignoring his mate's bark of surprise, he swung his human into his arms and carried him to the bedroom.

Chapter Four

Well, damn. He really can carry me.

Of course, knowing Eban was a shifter of some kind, Graham understood why. He still wasn't certain about the whole bonding right away thing, but he didn't bother fighting the big male as he carried him into his bedroom. With his brother's encouragement, he decided to just go with it.

Besides, I haven't had sex in over a year.

Graham's cock ached behind the fly of his jeans. With the way he was being held, carried bridal style, it was constricted almost painfully. When Eban laid him on the bed, the straightening of his body caused a relieved sigh to slip from his lips.

Eban headed back to the door and closed it, then turned to face him. A hungry smile curved his lips as he swept his gaze over Graham. He even licked his lips.

Deciding to take Eban at his word, which was easy when Graham spotted the swollen bulge at his groin, he rested his hands under his head. "See something you like?"

Growling softly, Eban stalked toward him. "You know that I do," he rumbled as he reached for the fly of his shorts. "I'm gonna make your body sing, Graham."

Graham felt his dick twitch when he heard the husky desire filling Eban's tone. His breath caught in his chest as his gaze riveted to the huge erection revealed when Eban kicked off his shorts and underwear. Obviously not at all shy about his body, Eban straightened, then crawled onto the bed, his massive rod jutting from him.

With his chute clenching, Graham felt his heart trip in his chest. "Damn. You're big," he whispered.

Eban had to be ten inches with a hefty girth.

"You'll be ready," Eban promised as he reached for Graham's shirt. "Let's get you more comfortable."

Graham allowed Eban to pull his shirt from his body. He paused after dropping the shirt over the side of the bed. When Eban stared for a moment, Graham had the unfamiliar urge to cover his chest. Even his skin flushed under his new lover's roving gaze.

"Gods, you're stunning, Graham," Eban purred, lowering his hands to his hips. "A fucking warrior's body."

Before Graham could come up with a response to that, Eban lowered his head and nuzzled his lips over his abdominals. He scraped his teeth over a scar on the left side of them. Then he pressed a kiss to it.

"Knife wound?" Eban guessed quietly.

Graham hummed in acknowledgment. "Five years ago."

Eban grunted, then skimmed his palms up his torso. Licking and nipping along Graham's flesh, he caused goose bumps to erupt over him. His nipples beaded, then tightened almost painfully when Eban licked over them.

Shifting restlessly on the bed, Graham groaned deep in his throat. "God, Eban," he muttered, sliding his fingers into the man's thick brown hair. He tugged it free of the hairband, allowing it to fall around the big man's chiseled features. "Hurry the fuck up, or I'm gonna come in my jeans."

Eban peered at Graham through his lashes as he licked over the puckered scar on the upper left pectoral. "Gunshot?"

Graham scowled at Eban. "You want to talk about my scars *now*?"

When Eban only arched one brow, Graham moaned.

"Yes," Graham confirmed. "I was shot three years ago on a mission."

Eban kissed the scar again, then lifted his head. "A warrior's body," he repeated with a smile as he swept his gaze over his torso once more. "Beautiful." Then Eban met Graham's gaze. "Lube?"

Graham had to think quickly.

Did he have any?

"Uhhh . . ." Graham grimaced, admitting, "I'm not sure. Jacking off really hasn't been a priority."

Eban pecked a kiss to his lips, then pushed off the bed. "I'll see what I can find."

While Eban rummaged first through the nightstand, then headed out of the room, probably to go into the bathroom, Graham sat up. He removed the boot and sock from his left foot. Unbuttoning his fly, Graham sighed at the release of pressure on his prick.

Then Graham shoved his jeans and underwear down and off, pushing them onto the floor.

Eban returned, closing the door behind him. He grinned as he prowled toward the bed, his gaze sweeping over him. With a lecherous smile on his face, Eban growled softly.

"I was getting to that," Eban claimed, climbing back on the bed.

Graham shrugged one shoulder. "Just helping us along since you had to go find lube." He felt his cheeks heat a little as Eban gripped his left thigh and pushed his legs wider. "Found some, then? Or lotion?"

"Snagged it from Cuzco's room."

Gaping, Graham froze.

Eban lifted his gaze from where he was petting Graham's right thigh. "What?" he asked in obvious confusion.

"You just went into my brother and his partner's room and found their lube?" Graham felt embarrassed for a whole new reason. "While naked?"

Smirking, Eban shook his head. "Shifters aren't shy about

nudity to begin with," he told him. "Besides, they're not home."

"Well—"

Then Eban lowered his head and buried his nose in Graham's pubes. He inhaled noisily, nudging his shaft with his cheek. His skin sliding over Graham's dick sent delicious tingles through his groin, and his cock twitched.

"You smell so fucking good, my mate," Eban told him before flicking out his tongue and sliding it over his crown.

Any thoughts of protest about where Eban had found the lube slipped right out of Graham's head. He could only stare at Eban as the man began mouthing kisses over his erection. His intense brown eyes peered back at him as he worked, telling him of the enjoyment he, too, was experiencing.

Just damn, he loves having his mouth on me.

"S-Suck me," Graham urged, his dick jerking beyond his control as another bead of pre-cum oozed from him. "Please."

Graham couldn't remember the last time he'd begged for anything, but right then, he needed so badly.

"With pleasure," Eban growled before opening his mouth and doing just that.

The feel of Eban's hot, wet mouth around his sensitive flesh tore a guttural groan from Graham. Arching, he pressed his head back into the comforter. His hands clenched in the fabric as the sweet suction created a cascade of pleasure to spread through his body.

Gritting his teeth, Graham trembled. His balls began to tighten embarrassingly fast. It had been far too long, and Eban's tongue was so very talented.

"E-Eban," Graham panted out. "C-Close."

Instead of pulling off, Eban hummed as he cradled his balls.

Graham barked a cry of pleasure as Eban hefted his testicles. They pulled tight, and his orgasm crashed through his body. Calling Eban's name, he pulsed spurt after spurt of cum

33

into Eban's still sucking mouth.

Floating on waves of endorphins—the sensations extended by Eban's ministrations—Graham sighed softly. He slowly came back to himself to feel the stretch in his ass. Peeling his eyelids open, he peered at his lover.

"Welcome back, handsome," Eban murmured, his face still nuzzling his groin. "Love the way you smell."

Figuring that was a shifter thing, Graham softly replied, "That's good."

Eban grinned up at him, then moved the fingers he had buried in Graham's chute.

Sparks erupted through Graham's groin as Eban teased over his prostate. He sucked in a sharp breath, meeting the other man's gaze.

"One more finger and you'll be ready," Eban stated with a growl. "Stay relaxed, my mate."

Then Eban returned to mouthing over Graham's groin, the jut of his hips, and around his cock. With his free hand, he reached up and tweaked his nipple. The hairs on Graham's arms stood on end as a fresh wave of arousal burned through his veins.

"Damn," Graham muttered, making certain to stay relaxed as he felt Eban pushing another finger into him. "H-How am I getting t-turned on again."

While Graham had never considered himself old at thirty-six, his days of back to back orgasms were well behind him. Except, he felt himself hardening once more even as a niggle of pain shot through his rectum.

"Breathe, my mate," Eban encouraged, stilling his digits within Graham. Rubbing his abdominals, he met his gaze. "You were made for me, Graham. Made for me to pleasure." Eban's brown eyes shown with an inner intensity. "Mine."

Graham felt as if his heart skipped a beat in his chest. He trembled under that gaze. His skin heated as a flush of . . .

something . . . worked through him.

Then Graham figured it out.

Longing.

After relying on his team for so long, then losing some of them only to end up alone, Graham wanted that connection again—needed it.

"Yeah." Graham swallowed hard, then went with it. "I'm yours."

Eban's shark roared in the back of his mind. He let out a feral growl as he began working his fingers again. His mate was nearly stretched enough, and he needed inside him so badly.

Finally, Eban understood when his pod-mates decided to do anything to win their mate. The fact that Graham knew about paranormals made it a little easier for him, but Eban knew it wouldn't all be roses. They still had so much to learn about each other.

But later.

Easing his fingers free of Graham's chute, Eban gripped his dick and wiped the remaining slick on it. At the same time, he levered over his human. His heart thundered with pleasure as Graham reached for him.

Eban rested his weight on his right hand. Gripping Graham's right thigh in his other hand, he lifted his human's still-healing leg. Recalling the irritated skin, Eban didn't want to run the risk of it rubbing on the blanket and bothering his lover.

Shifting his hips, Eban nudged his cock head to Graham's prepared hole. He pushed, watching his crown sink past his mate's guardian muscle. Slick heat wrapped around him, causing his gut to clench.

Fighting back his instinct to slam home and claim what was his, Eban paused. He lifted his gaze and focused on Graham's face. Seeing the lines of tension there, he lowered his head and pressed a kiss to his human's lips.

"Relax," Eban urged before nipping Graham's bottom lip.

Graham opened to him, and Eban slid his tongue inside. He slowly mapped his mouth anew, taking his time. Noticing the slight relaxing of the muscles around his cock head, he eased more of himself inside as he continued to enjoy Graham's mouth.

Eban fed Graham a moan as more and more of his erection became sheathed in hot bliss. His gut clenched as he stilled, finally fully seated. Balls deep in his mate for the first time, Eban lifted his head and stared in wonder at the man Fate had deemed his.

"Mine," Eban murmured, nuzzling his cheek against Graham's. "My handsome warrior."

Groaning, Graham rubbed his hands up and down Eban's back. "Not a warrior anymore," he mumbled as he shifted his hips, obviously searching for friction.

Growling low in his throat, Eban gave Graham what they both wanted. He began to ease his hips backward. "You're still a warrior," he purred into his mate's ear. "Your injury doesn't change that."

Then Eban adjusted the angle of his hips and drove back into Graham. To his delight, his lover cried out, the sound one of pleasure. Eban kept at that angle as he sped up his rutting, giving Graham as much stimulation as he could.

Eban scraped his canines over the flesh of Graham's shoulder. His teeth extended in preparation for his bite. He barely refrained, wanting to drive his lover out of his mind with bliss.

"Grab your dick, mate," Eban ordered gruffly. "Jack yourself and come. I want to feel your chute ripple along my length."

Feeling one of Graham's hands move from his back to between their bodies, Eban knew he'd obeyed. Only three thrusts later, he felt his human's body tense. A shudder went through the strong frame beneath him.

"O-Oh fuck, Eb," Graham moaned into his ear. "I-I'm going—" His words ended on a long, low groan.

"Yessss," Eban snarled, reveling in the clench and release on his cock. "So sexy when you come."

Eban drove in deep one last time and stopped fighting his heavy balls' need for release. Relishing the sweet feel of his orgasm, he moaned in Graham's ear. His hips pressed firmly against his mate's ass as he poured his seed into the other man.

Giving in to instinct, Eban sank his canines deep into the flesh where Graham's neck met his shoulder. He sucked at the bite, drawing his mate's life-giving fluid into his mouth. Rolling the iron-rich blood across his tongue, he hummed appreciatively before swallowing.

Graham grunted as a shiver worked through his body.

After another couple of sucks, Eban eased his teeth free of Graham. He licked over the wound. A smile curving his lips, he stared at his mark.

"You look really pleased with yourself."

Eban turned upon hearing Graham's slightly slurred words and found him staring at him, a loopy-looking smile on his flushed face. He found he loved that expression. Easing his grip on Graham's thigh, Eban gently lowered his leg. He brought his now empty hand up and traced around Graham's jaw.

"I am pleased with myself," Eban admitted. "I claimed my mate. Nothing could possibly be better than seeing your blissed-out expression. My gorgeous warrior."

Graham's face took on a slightly darker hue, and Eban scented his mate's mild embarrassment. That wasn't what he wanted. Pecking a kiss to Graham's lips, Eban lifted away from him, carefully easing his softening shaft from his lover.

Hearing Graham grunt, Eban returned his attention to his face. He saw his lover shift his hips a little as his lips pinched at the sides. His eyes narrowed, too.

"Are you okay?" Eban asked, concerned he'd hurt his human mate. "I wasn't too rough on you, was I?"

Graham shook his head. "I'm fine. Just—" He cleared his throat as he glanced down between them. "Never done it without a rubber. Didn't expect—"

Eban quickly eased from the bed. "I'll get something to clean us up," he told him. After pressing another kiss to Graham's lips, Eban whispered, "Thank you."

Smirking, Graham asked, "Shouldn't I be saying that to you?"

Chuckling, Eban headed to the bathroom.

CHAPTER FIVE

"Eban asked me to move in with him," Graham admitted, tapping his beer bottle with his forefinger.

Grisham turned from where he stood at the stove, cooking a stir-fry. "I'm surprised he waited this long."

Graham took a sip of his beer before returning it to the table. "We've only known each other five days."

Snorting, Grisham shrugged. "Paranormals do things fast. We know this." Arching one brow, he stated, "You're his mate. He wants you with him. It really is as simple as that."

Nodding slowly, Graham felt the wheels in his brain churning. "I guess it's human to have doubts, especially since he hasn't shown me his shark, yet."

"He hasn't shown you his great white?" Grisham sounded surprised. "Why?"

Graham snorted. "Said he was worried I'd be afraid of him."

Grisham scoffed derisively, easily expressing exactly what he thought of that.

"Right?" Graham leaned back in his chair. "Guess I don't want to move in with him if he doesn't trust me with something so important."

"Tell him."

Heaving a sigh, Graham nodded. "That whole communication thing in a relationship. Forgot about that."

"You've never been in a relationship," Grisham pointed out. "So not surprising you wouldn't always remember."

Graham heard the front door of their condo open and close,

telling him Cuzco had gotten home from work. He'd had a shift in the aquarium in his octopus form. Graham still found it fascinating to think that many of the people working at *World of Aquatica* were actually aquatic or semi-aquatic shifters.

Hell, the tiger sharks are all shifters. No wonder they can put on a show.

"Hey, babe," Grisham called when Cuzco didn't automatically appear. "Everything okay?"

"Um." Cuzco finally rounded the corner. He paused and glanced between them. "No."

Grisham lowered the heat on the stir-fry, set down the wooden spoon he'd been using, and headed toward his partner. "What's going on? What's wrong?"

Cuzco heaved a sigh before accepting a cuddle and kiss from Grisham. Then he turned a troubled expression Graham's way. "Two things, actually." Cuzco pointed at him. "First, seriously. Not that it hasn't been nice having you here, but just move in with Eban already. The tension in his shark is driving us all nuts."

Graham barked a laugh as he rolled his eyes. "I'll talk to him about it again," he promised before taking a drink of his beer.

"And second?" Grisham pressed.

Holding up a piece of paper Graham hadn't noticed, Cuzco waved it a little. "How come you didn't tell us you have a stalker?"

Graham just fought off wincing as Grisham grabbed the paper and read it. Sighing deeply, he frowned at his beer. He could guess what Grisham was reading, and he didn't want to see the expression on his brother's face while doing it.

"Graham?" Grisham muttered. "What the fuck?"

Lifting his gaze to Grisham, Graham raised his hand only to return it to the table. "I don't know who's sending them. What was the point?"

Graham knew that was the wrong thing to say as soon as the words were out of his mouth.

Grisham's face darkened with anger as he surged forward. After tossing the letter on the table, thankfully folded so Graham didn't catch the words, he rested his knuckles on it. He leaned forward and scowled at him.

"Whoever this yahoo is is threatening you," Grisham pointed out.

"I never go anywhere but the marine park. With all the security, I'm perfectly safe," Graham countered, frowning. When that didn't seem to appease his brother, he quickly added, "And Eban knows. He's having his people look into it."

Grisham's shoulders sagged, and he dropped into a seat. "You trusted him with it, but not me?"

Cuzco settled on his lap, his arms around Grisham's shoulders, and Grisham held him close.

Graham bet Cuzco did that to soothe his obviously upset brother.

Damn. Didn't mean to do that.

"Any answer I give you, you're not going to like, so I'm going to go with the painful truth." Graham wrapped both hands around the bottle and rested his forearms on the table. "You know when I first started recovery, I didn't think I deserved to be one of the guys who'd survived."

Grisham nodded. "You suffered from survivor's guilt."

Graham nodded, too. "Right. At the time when those letters started, I still felt that way. I thought—" He hesitated, worried about the reaction he was about to receive, but knew he needed to push on. "Well, I thought I deserved to have someone off me, since I shouldn't have lived anyway."

"God, Graham," Grisham whispered, his complexion paling. He shook his head, opened his mouth, then closed it again.

Lifting one hand, Graham assured, "I no longer feel that

way, but since I was here and never saw anyone, I didn't really feel like it was an issue." He shrugged. "I took your words to heart." When Graham saw Grisham's tilted head and confused expression, he explained, "I've ordered a sports prosthesis, so before I begin going anywhere where a stalker might be, I'll be prepared. I *am* ex-military and can take care of myself."

Grisham rubbed a hand over his face, obviously still struggling with Graham's decision. Sighing, he lowered his hand and stared at him. "Then why tell Eban?" Grisham pointed a finger at him. "And I completely disagree with your decision of thinking you're safe." Tapping the note, he stated, "This guy knows shit he shouldn't."

Graham almost reached for the note, but he hesitated. Enough people had handled it already. "I had one come the day we met, and he opened it and read it." Cocking his head, Graham focused on Cuzco. "Not that I'm upset, but why did you open my mail?"

Cuzco's pale features took on a pinkish hue. "It was a mistake. I didn't pay close enough attention to the name on the front, and I thought it was for your brother." Nibbling his bottom lip, he told him, "We open each other's mail all the time."

Grisham nodded.

Makes sense.

Eban growled low in his throat, anger surging through him. "The stalker was in the park."

The newest note had included a line about how even Graham's *new big fag protector couldn't save him.* That meant someone had seen his mate with him in the park. They'd shared lunch every day, so it could have been any time during the week.

"Or someone they hired to spy on me," Graham pointed out.

Tightening his arm around Graham's shoulders—they were sitting on a small sofa together in Alpha Kaiser's large office—Eban narrowed his eyes. "Stalkers don't normally work with other people, but maybe."

"Your notes are about how you didn't deserve to come back," Captain John Casinov mused. The man was the mate of their pod's beta—William Roush—and headed up the precinct where Grisham worked. "Do you think it's specific to your last deployment when you were injured?"

"That seems the logical assumption," Graham replied slowly, narrowing his eyes. "Prior to that assignment, it had been four years since we lost any member of our team."

Graham rubbed at his chest as if in pain from the memory, and Eban leaned over and nuzzled his neck, doing his best to soothe his human. To his relief, his mate flashed a smile his way.

Eban straightened as he listened to Beta William state, "That's where we start then." Since Alpha Kaiser was in San Diego with his mate, Arthur, for business reasons, the beta was in charge. "Ovram, dig up everything you can on the family of all the soldiers who fell during Graham's last mission." William turned his attention to Graham. "Can you give us their names?"

"Uh, isn't that classified?" John pointed out. "Won't it bring trouble from the military onto you?"

William winked at his mate. "Don't worry. Ovram won't get caught."

John ran a hand through his graying brown hair. "Maybe I shouldn't have sat in on this meeting."

Threading his fingers with his mate's, William leveled a serious gaze on him. "I'll never purposefully keep stuff from you, my mate. And this wouldn't fall in your jurisdiction even if Ovram did get caught."

Sighing, John nodded. "Of course, you're right." The pair

leaned close and exchanged a short kiss.

"Don't worry, guys. I won't get caught," Ovram claimed with a grin. He cracked his knuckles. "Just get me that list, Graham, and I'll get on it."

"You should reach out to the other survivors and find out if they're getting threatening letters, too," Grisham told him. "We need to know if it's just you being targeted, bro."

Graham nodded. "Will do." Although, from his scent, he didn't look too happy about doing it.

"Did you ever hear back from Price?" Eban asked curiously, knowing Graham had sent him an email a couple of days ago.

Shaking his head, Graham told him, "He's probably deployed and can't check messages right now. I don't expect to hear from him for a week or two."

"So, you and the vampire and one other survived?" Ovram asked.

Grimacing, Graham nodded. "Yeah. We lost three men on the mission." He gave Ovram the names, all the while rubbing his right thigh, betraying his unease.

"After getting a list of family and friends of these guys, I'm going to cross-reference with anyone who purchased a ticket to the marine park using a credit card over the last week," Ovram told them, typing on the table sitting on his knee. "It's a long shot, but you never know."

"Thanks, Ov," Eban told him. "I appreciate it." Then he turned and gave his mate a beseeching look. "So, now will you move in with me?"

Graham arched one brow as he peered back at him. "Will you show me your shark?"

Eban tightened his lips a little before saying, "Great whites ended up getting such a bad rap due to all those shark movies."

"Yeah, but you're not some random great white," Graham

pointed out. "You're Eban. Like you said, you're still sentient while in animal form."

"You haven't introduced him to your animal, yet?" William asked, his brows creasing. "Go do that, Eban." He shook his head. "No wonder your shark has been so restless these last few days. I thought it was just because you hadn't gone swimming for a while, but now I know you've been denying him contact with his mate." Rising to his feet, William drew John with him. "Anything we can help you with, Ovram?"

Ovram shook his head as he stood, too. "Naw. I got this." Then the sea lion shifter stood and headed out of the office.

"Come on, my mate." Eban rose to his feet and held out his hand. "We'll go to the grotto."

To Eban's pleasure, Graham placed his hand in Eban's and allowed him to help him to his feet.

"After that, you can help me move my meager belongings to your condo," Graham told him, getting his balance on his cane. He didn't seem to use it as often, having become much better accustomed to his prosthesis, but he still carried it. Waggling his eyebrows, Graham grinned at him, "And since I missed dinner due to this impromptu meeting, you can cook for me."

Eban chuckled softly as they followed the others out of the room. "You have a deal."

"So, what's the grotto?" Graham asked.

"A massive underground lake," Eban told him. "There's a passage that connects to the ocean. During high tide, it's underwater." Turning left, he guided him away from the others and toward an elevator. "We have special sensors buried around that area to keep it hidden from radar and satellites."

"Wow. How do you get away with that?"

Eban pushed the button to call the elevator before winking at Graham. "I have no fucking clue how Ovram has it set up and still don't call attention to ourselves." He shrugged as the doors opened. "I should have warned you before that I suck with tech shit." Then Eban guided Graham inside the car.

Graham chuckled as he nodded. "So, why hide the area around the tunnel?"

Hitting the C button to send the car heading down, Eban told him, "Because there are shifters here that turn into animals that humans think are extinct."

"Really? Like what?"

"You've met Tyrone, right? One of my security guys?" After Graham nodded, Eban continued, "He turns into this huge thirty-five-foot Steller's sea cow. They were supposed to have gone extinct over a hundred years ago."

"Wow." Graham hummed. "I'd love to see that."

Recalling a second shifter, Eban stated, "And I doubt you've met him yet, but Rawlins shares his spirit with an ammonite, which is a type of extinct mollusk. His blue-green and yellow shell is absolutely breathtaking."

Graham made another impressed sound, but the noise quickly died away due to the elevator doors opening. A second later, he stepped out, grabbed the railing, and let out a low whistle.

Eban chuckled, standing beside him on the platform. "Impressive, right?"

Nodding, Graham peered around the place. Eban watched as his mate took in the giant underground cavern. There were several dozen steps leading from the platform the elevator opened onto, ending at a sandy beach. The hidden lake lapped over the granules, darkening some of it.

"Come on," Eban urged, turning him toward the steps. "How are you doing with stairs on your new leg?"

Graham shrugged. "Slow."

Eban nodded, then began leading the way down.

"How come you don't have the elevator take you the rest of the way down?"

Keeping part of his attention on his slow-moving mate, Eban replied, "Because during storm season, the water in here can get that high. We've even had the elevator shaft flood a time or two."

"Damn," Graham whispered. "Sounds like a lot of water."

Nodding in silent agreement, Eban ordered, "Don't come down here in inclement weather, please."

Graham paused on the last step. "You'll get no argument from me." Then he grimaced before focusing on Eban. "At the risk of sounding unmanly, I'm not certain how I'll do on the sand. Can I hold your hand?"

Pleasure flooded Eban that Graham was willing to ask for his help. "I don't need an excuse to hold your hand," he told him, hoping to ease his mate's uncertainty while offering his hand.

"Thanks," Graham murmured, taking his hand.

Eban helped Graham off the last step, helping him become steady with the shifting sand under his feet. After a few steps, he seemed to catch his balance. To Eban's pride, Graham didn't let go of his hand.

CHAPTER SIX

"Uh, I guess we didn't plan this very well," Graham commented as he stared at the water, then his prosthesis, then back at the water. Focusing on Eban, he stated, "Should I assume I would need to get pretty deep to see your shark?"

Humming, Eban nodded. "I have an idea, though."

Eban released Graham's hand, and he found him instantly missing the contact.

Huh. Must be a mate thing.

As Graham watched, Eban started stripping. Smirking, he stated, "Not that I don't find the view fantastic, but—" He groaned. "Right, shifting requires no clothes."

Winking, Eban pointed at Graham's clothes. "Still don't know why you insist on wearing briefs, but I guess they'll come in handy for swimming with me. You strip, too, then take off your prosthesis."

"Uh, then how will I get in the water?" Graham asked dubiously. "Hop? Crawl? Cause that ain't happening."

Not in this lifetime.

Eban shook his head, still grinning. "Naw. I'll carry you in and out. Don't worry." He stepped close and cupped Graham's jaw, his expression turning serious. "I'll take good care of you, my mate." After that declaration, Eban pressed his lips to Graham's in a much too short kiss before pulling away and shoving off his shorts.

Graham pushed down his immediate knee-jerk reaction to refuse. Ignoring his pride, he nodded instead. "Yeah. Okay." He did want to swim with the shark, after all.

Dropping his cane, Graham grabbed the hem of his shirt. He whipped it over his head, then folded it and placed it on the dry sand. His fingers went to the fly of his jeans, but spotting Eban's naked body stalled his movements.

His big and broad lover was a thing of beauty, scars and all. He'd licked every bit of his shifter's puckered flesh over the last few days. Eban returned the favor and did the same to his own, settling his concerns that his lover would be turned off by them.

"If you keep looking at me, I'm going to fuck you on this beach, and we're not going to get to swimming for some time."

Graham groaned upon hearing Eban's gruffly spoken words. His blood flowed south, and his chute clenched. Then his stomach rumbled.

Eban chuckled. "Hurry up, handsome."

Nodding, Graham swiftly undid his jeans and shoved them down his legs . . . only to lose his balance and, with a surprised yelp, began to topple.

"Easy, Graham," Eban called as his big, strong arms wrapped around his torso. "Let's have you sit down first."

Graham blew out an embarrassed breath even as he allowed Eban to guide him to the ground. "Geez, that was dumb." Once upon a time, Graham wouldn't have had any trouble removing his jeans on a beach.

Those days are long gone.

Sitting on the sand, Graham watched as Eban removed his footwear, then the rest of his clothes, leaving him in his underwear.

"One of these days, I'm going to have you teach me how to put that thing on and off of you," Eban told him from where he knelt beside him.

As Graham removed his leg, he furrowed his brows. "Why would you need to know how to do that?"

Eban shrugged. "Because I like taking care of you."

Graham figured it was as simple as that. The man was a shifter and had a different set of instincts. In fact, they were instincts that Graham was becoming appreciative of.

"Okay." Graham set his leg on his pile of clothes. "Ready."

Sliding his arms around Graham's back and knees, Eban easily lifted him. He still found himself shocked at his lover's strength. The way he handled himself never failed to give Graham a boner.

Fortunately, Eban always seemed happy to take care of it, too.

Just thinking about sex had a predictable reaction on his body. His blood rushed to his prick, and he began to thicken.

Eban growled softly. "Hopefully, this water will help us with our problems," he grumbled, frowning. "I hate leaving you hangin', my mate."

"I can't help it when I'm in your arms," Graham admitted. Never before had he thought such sappiness would cross his lips.

"Good." Eban gave him a swift kiss, then took them deeper.

When the cold water hit Graham's foot, then his ass, he hissed. Once his body was half-submerged, his burgeoning erection died a swift death. He figured that was a good thing, though.

"Okay, I'm gonna put you on your feet." Eban winced. "Uh, foot?"

Graham laughed softly. "The fact that you forgot . . . actually warms me a little bit."

Eban grinned, then kissed him again. His tongue lingered in Graham's mouth, and he welcomed the play.

With a groan, Eban tore his mouth away from Graham's. "Ugh. You're so fucking sexy and distracting."

Winking, Graham stated, "Well, I guess you better let me meet your shark so we can get back to some other fun stuff."

Nodding, Eban carefully placed him down.

Graham easily caught his balance, moving his arms through the water and floating. Swimming during therapy had always been a favorite. Hearing splashing, Graham spotted Eban moving farther away.

"Remember, Graham," Eban stated, treading water ten feet away. "You're perfectly safe with my shark."

"I know, Eban," Graham replied, trying to soothe his worried lover. Never would he have thought the big confident man would have such fears, and he wanted to help put them to rest. "It's still you. I know that. Stop worrying."

Eban nodded. Then he sank under the water. Bubbles broke the surface as the water churned. After a few seconds, there was nothing.

Graham swept his gaze around the cavern, searching. Finally, thirty feet to his left, a fin broke the surface of the water. He sucked in a surprised gasp, shocked at how huge it was.

"Damn," Graham whispered, staring intently.

The fin moved left, then right, making figure eights in the water, but it never drew closer, even after several minutes.

Reminding himself of his vow to assuage Eban's fears, Graham began swimming slowly toward the circling shark. To his relief, the animal didn't try to get farther away. He reached his shifter's shark and brushed his palm over the animal's side as it swam past.

On the next pass, Graham kicked with his arms and legs and lunged upward. He brought his hands up and managed to grab onto his dorsal fin. The shark sank a little lower in the water, allowing Graham to get more comfortable hanging onto his back.

Then the shark sped up.

Graham laughed as his body cut through the water at an impressive rate. Waves rippled around him. The feeling of freedom surged through him, and Graham realized swimming with his shark was going to become a favorite activity.

Examining the creature, Graham realized he had to be at least eighteen feet long. Even in shark form, there was considerable scarring on his right side in front of his fin. In fact, he could easily see how Eban must have fought off another large shark.

After fifteen minutes, Graham's arms grew tired. When they made another pass near the beach, he let go. His body slowed, and he moved to his back, floating.

A few minutes later, Eban, in human form, swam next to him. "You doing okay?" he asked.

Grinning at his lover, Graham nodded. "Oh, yeah. Thank you, Eban. That was amazing."

"No, thank *you*," Eban countered, threading their fingers together. "I'm sorry it took me so long to shift for you."

Graham squeezed Eban's fingers. "You were worried." With a wink, he added, "And I'm gonna wanna do that a lot. That was fun."

Eban growled softly. "Hell, yeah. Anytime, my mate."

With his body reacting to his lover's rumbling words, Graham felt his prick begin to thicken, despite the cold water. "Come to shore with me," he urged, sweeping his gaze over Eban's naked form. He could just make out the bobbing of the handsome man's half-hard prick. "I want to suck you."

Drawing in a harsh gasp, Eban widened his eyes.

Graham winked. "Surprised?" He returned his focus to Eban's cock, seeing that the crown now bobbed out of the water. He heard Eban groan, and as Graham watched, his lover's cock thickened further. "You like that idea."

Eban turned in the water and wrapped his arms around Graham's waist. "Of course I like that idea. I love having you any way I can get you."

Wrapping his arms around Eban's neck, Graham began

sucking up a mark on his man's neck as he carried them both to shore.

Wading to shore, Eban rested one hand on Graham's ass and the other on his hip. He reveled in the way his human had latched his mouth onto his neck tendon. The sucking seemed to transfer straight to his cock, and he twitched and leaked against Graham's beautiful hard mound he palmed.

"W-We're to shore," Eban mumbled roughly, his pulse pounding through his veins. "N-Now what do you want, my mate?"

Graham lifted his head and gave him a lazy smile. "Lie down in the sand, lover," he ordered, his gaze hot and heavy. "I'm gonna suck you so hard and drink your seed."

Groaning, Eban nodded as he turned and slowly lowered them both to the ground. He didn't release Graham until they were both on their knees. Then, when his mate pushed at his torso, Eban easily went with the movement.

Eban flopped onto his back, uncaring of the sand getting into all his cracks. Instead, he watched intently as Graham straddled his thighs. Then he cupped Eban's balls and pulled them upward, so they were cradled in the vee of his thighs. His cock arched over his stomach, beads of pre-cum sliding across his glans.

"Damn, Eban," Graham muttered appreciatively. "Look at your cock. Can't believe I managed to take that in my ass."

Graham gently gripped his erection. He slid his palm up and down his length in a slow, light jacking. It wasn't enough, not nearly enough, but it also felt so damn good.

Digging his fingers into the sand on either side of him, Eban watched as Graham fondled him. His mate used one hand to hold his erection, pointing it at the stone ceiling. With his other hand, he massaged his pre-cum into his crown.

When Eban's dick pulsed another bead, Graham slid it down and rubbed it into his frenulum.

Moaning raggedly, Eban bucked his hips before he could get hold of himself.

Giving him a wicked grin, Graham asked, "Need something?"

Eban groaned and shuddered. "Y-You said you were going to suck me," he pointed out, a hint of neediness in his tone that he would forever deny. "Instead, y-you t-tease."

"Pleasure," Graham countered. "Enjoying touching you." He finally scooched back a little on his knees. "Like you enjoy touching me." Bending at the waist, Graham met Eban's gaze. "Licking your fluids and"—he stroked him slowly with one hand—"milking you for more."

Moaning once more, Eban nodded. "D-Do love seeing you p-playing with m-me."

Graham flashed a broad grin his way, then stuck out his tongue and swiped it over Eban's flared cap.

Eban trembled, digging his hands deeper into the sand. He fought the urge to wrap his fingers around Graham's skull and pull him down. His desire to fuck his mate's mouth burned through his veins, but he kept his hands to himself.

With a lascivious smile, Graham winked. Then he barely parted his lips and began placing sucking kisses all over his cap. He even took a few seconds to suckle the wrinkled skin beneath.

"By the gods," Eban ground out, barely controlling his hips. "More. Oh, fuck! More."

"Love hearing you beg," Graham claimed. Then he opened his mouth and swallowed Eban to the root.

Eban howled deeply and lost control of his hips. Bucking up, he nearly shoved his mate off of him.

Graham quickly recovered, placing his hands in the sand on either side of him. As Eban's ass returned to the ground, he sucked strongly. The pressure sent a surge of heat straight to his balls.

Unable to help himself, Eban popped his hips up again. That time, Graham took him into the back of his throat easily. He even swallowed around his crown, causing goose bumps to break out on his groin.

"G-Graham! Mate!"

Eban couldn't stop himself from doing it over and over. He stared at his lover, enraptured by the sight of him accepting his dick between his lips. His prick gleamed in the low lighting of the cavern, and spittle oozed from between Graham's lips even as he managed to swallow around his crown.

Lost in sensation, Eban felt his balls draw up. He opened his mouth to warn his lover, but it was too late. With a cry of bliss, he arched and shot.

His senses singing, Eban lost himself to the throes of ecstasy caused by his release. He reveled in the feel of his cum spurting, his balls tingling, and his gut clenching. The waves of bliss lapped at his mind, and his body trembled.

Eban wasn't certain how long he lay there, flying on the high of his endorphins. Eventually, he recognized the feel of petting on his abdominals. He peeled open eyelids he didn't remember closing and spotted Graham resting his cheek on his thigh.

"Wow, Graham," Eban mumbled, meeting his eyes. He offered him a sated smile. "Should I be jealous of whoever taught you those skills?"

Graham chuckled, the sound husky, probably from Eban repeatedly burying his dick in his throat. Smirking up at him, he muttered, "The first time you sucked me off, I thought the very same thing."

Snickering softly, Eban winked. "Fair enough." Then he heard Graham's stomach gurgle, and he moaned as he pulled his hand out of the sand and rubbed it over Graham's skull.

The man didn't even seem to mind that sand was getting on him. "You just sucked the life out of me," Eban whined. "And now I gotta figure out how to move."

"Would it help if I reminded you that you're going to help me move in with you?" Graham asked, a twinkle in his eyes.

Eban grinned broadly as he eased into a sitting position. "That'll do it."

As Graham laughed, Eban moved them back to the underground lake to clean the sand from their bits before he helped his mate with his leg and getting dressed.

CHAPTER SEVEN

Graham groaned as he eased to a sitting position. Swinging his legs over the side of the bed, he winced. As much as he loved the feel of Eban's cock splitting him wide open, three times in one night was evidently one too many.

Grabbing his crutches, Graham hobbled to the bathroom. He had every intention of lounging in the tub for a half-hour with salts before starting his day. As he passed the dresser, he snagged his phone, intending to text Eban to see where his missing lover was.

Once Graham started the bath and poured in the salts, he turned his attention to his morning routine. He pissed, washed up, and brushed his teeth. Finally, he set his crutches against the wall and sank into the massive jetted tub.

Heaven.

Relaxing against the back of the tub, Graham grabbed his phone and began composing his text. The sound of the door-knob turning caught his attention. He smiled as he watched Eban stride into the room, but his gaze remained riveted on the steaming mugs he held as opposed to his lover's ripped abdominals since he only wore sweatpants.

Eban chuckled softly as he crouched beside the tub and held out one cup. When Graham reached for it, he pulled it back. "Ah, ah, ah," he teased. "First things first."

Graham rolled his eyes but couldn't help smiling at the man. "Good morning, Eban," he greeted, then puckered his lips.

Humming, Eban leaned forward and pressed his mouth to

Graham's. He slid his tongue into him and began a thorough exploration. Graham welcomed it, enjoying the flavor of Eban, coffee, and something sweet.

Hmmm.

When Eban broke the kiss and lifted his head, he smiled and held out the coffee. "Good morning, Graham."

Chuckling softly, Graham took the mug and brought it to his lips. He inhaled deeply, enjoying the scent of coffee and sugar. His lover had laughed when he'd learned Graham's coffee preference, but he made it for him anyway.

"With four sugars?" Eban had shaken his head with a mock scowl. "I thought you military types all took it black."

Graham had snorted. "Of course I can drink it black, but if I have a choice? Why the hell would I?"

Eban had just laughed.

As Graham relaxed in the tub, letting the bath salts do their work, he met Eban's eyes. His man swept his gaze over him, his expression one of concern. Graham waited, knowing his lover would ask before too long.

Sitting on the closed lid of the toilet, Eban held his own mug of coffee and rested his forearms on his thighs. "I was too rough with you last night, wasn't I?" He rubbed his chest while furrowing his brows. "Just wanted you so damn much, I—"

"Hey." Graham reached out and touched his hand, getting his attention. "You didn't do anything I didn't desperately want you to. Got it?"

Eban nodded slowly, not looking convinced.

Leaning forward, Graham grabbed Eban's wrist. "Truthfully." He gave his lover a hard look. "I will tell you if I ever don't like something, and if I ever need you to stop, I will tell you that, too." Waving at the bathwater, Graham stated, "This will make me good as new, especially with that nifty increased healing I got from bonding with you."

58

That had certainly made his recovery and his body's acceptance of his prosthesis so much easier. His balance had become much better, and his stump scars were well on the way to never hurting. He'd even had to stop using the veteran's medical facilities, since there would be no way to explain everything.

Of course, since there was a doctor on staff in the shifter pod—a hammerhead shifter named Anthony—he didn't even need medical insurance anymore.

"Okay," Eban rumbled. "I'll take you at your word."

"Good." After taking a sip and relaxing in the tub once more, Graham winked. "And I really do like how you insist we greet each other in the morning when we're both here."

Sometimes, Eban was already at work, having been called in for something to do with their shifter pod. He was their head enforcer, after all. He supported his alpha, beta, and their pod in whatever way was necessary. Not only that, but he was head of security for the marine park, which meant he was in charge of scheduling everyone under him and following up on incidents. His shifter was a busy man.

"You make it worth it," Eban murmured as he leaned forward and pecked another kiss to Graham's lips. Then he straightened. "Did the doc tell you when you'd be cleared for duty?"

Graham had been offered a place in Eban's security at the park. He'd learned that, after someone mated with a shifter in the pod, they would often join the park staff in some capacity. It didn't always happen—hence John and Grisham still being cops—but quite a few did.

In Graham's case, he was happy to pull his weight.

"According to Doc Anthony, I'll probably be able to handle four-hour shifts in another week," Graham replied before taking another sip of his coffee. He hummed appreciatively, loving how Eban had put in just the right amount of sugar.

"Where are you putting me first?"

Over the last two weeks of living with Eban, he'd spent hours exploring the park—both the upfront portions as well as the behind the scenes stuff. The way the shifters hid everything was fascinating. He couldn't imagine keeping track of all the hidden pipes and tubing which allowed the shifters in and out of their aquariums.

"I'm going to pair you with Dare first," Eban told him. "You'll be patrolling the park." After a sip of his own coffee, he added, "Dare will explain how we decide to adjust rotations so we never become predictable." Eban winked. "Don't want to make it easy for pick-pockets or their ilk."

Graham nodded, accepting that. Not only would it help to continue to rehabilitate him—walking slowly—being with Dare would keep him safe from his stalker. Well, that was assuming Eban's people wouldn't figure out who it was first.

So far, Graham had received six more letters.

They're increasing in frequency.

At least whoever it is doesn't know about my new condo number.

"I-I'm sorry." Graham's brows were lifted, his surprise clear. "You want to do . . . what?"

Eban didn't miss a beat. "Put an announcement for our upcoming nuptials in the paper."

Graham licked his lips as his brows ratcheted up a little higher. "Yeah," he murmured, rubbing the back of his neck. "That's what I thought you said."

"Damn. A little old school, but that will definitely get your stalker's attention," Grisham commented from a different sofa, Cuzco next to him.

They were once again gathered in Alpha Kaiser's large study. That time, their alpha was in attendance, however. The formidable man relaxed on another sofa with Arthur at his side.

William and John had settled on a pair of comfortable chairs, as had Ovram.

Then Graham smirked over at Eban. "Sure, handsome. When you decide to propose, we'll put an ad about it out in whatever paper you want."

Eban felt heat sting his cheeks.

Oops.

A second later, Eban dropped to his knees. He knee-walked toward Graham, placing his hands on his mate's knees. Then he peered up into his clearly surprised human's expression.

"My dear mate," Eban began racking his mind for the right words. "You mean more to me than my own life. You are my heart and soul." Rubbing up and down Graham's thighs, Eban told him, "I admit I don't understand how the restrictions around human marriage can be so important to some, because the divorce rate is so high, but I would be honored to enter into that sacred union, so every non-paranormal in the world will know that I am yours and you are mine." Eban eased even closer, pressing between his thighs. "Will you do me the honor of marrying me?"

"Damn," Graham whispered as he rested his hands on Eban's shoulders. "Yeah. Yeah, I'll marry you." Then he cocked his head as his brows furrowed in a worried look. "You've been alive for centuries. Is Eban even your real name? Do you even have an identity to marry me?"

Ovram barked out a laugh as Eban crushed Graham to his chest. He captured his mate's mouth in a kiss that instantly went feral. Sweeping his tongue between Graham's lips, he teased, licked, and mapped all over again.

Only the sound of his alpha calling his name pulled Eban from his need. He ended the kiss and glanced around. No one looked his way save Ovram, who was smirking at him while palming his crotch.

Eban growled at the male.

Shrugging one shoulder negligently, Ovram just continued to smile at him.

Huffing an annoyed sigh, Eban returned his focus to a slightly dazed-looking Graham.

"Yeah, I don't need to see my older brother making out like that ever again."

Eban ignored Grisham's comment in favor of cradling Graham's jaw. He teased his thumb along his kiss-swollen lips. The move drew his mate's attention, blinking twice to focus on him.

"Yes, Eban is my real name, although I wasn't always O'Gillie," he admitted with a shrug. "I didn't have a sir name two hundred years ago. Shifters didn't bother until it became required for blending in with proper society."

"Okay." Graham turned his head and pressed a kiss to his palm before murmuring, "And an actual identity."

"Don't worry, Graham," Ovram spoke up. "I got everyone here covered. Your marriage will appear legal and binding to every institution that looks into it."

Graham nodded again. "Okay. Good. I don't want to draw attention to us to draw out a stalker."

"We're covered," Eban assured as he eased back into his seat. Wrapping his arms around Graham, he kept a close hold on him, unable to release his mate just yet.

"Okay, soooo, now that that is out of the way," William commented, his tone clearly teasing. "The article about your upcoming nuptials is only step one."

Even while allowing himself to be cuddled against Eban's side, Graham asked, "Okay. What's step two?"

Alpha Kaiser chuckled low in his throat. "How do you feel about tuxedos?"

Graham frowned. "You mean . . . like at our wedding?" He scoffed as he glanced Eban's way. "Now, there's something I never thought I'd say."

"Never thought about getting married?" Eban asked curiously.

Shaking his head, Graham admitted, "No. Never thought about getting married. I was career military. Remember?"

"Right." Eban nodded. Then another thought stabbed into his brain, and he peered down at his human. "Am I smothering you?"

Barking a laugh, Graham asked, "You're just wondering about that now? We've been together for weeks."

Eban grimaced. "I've never been in a relationship before."

Sobering, Graham smiled at him kindly as he rubbed over Eban's shoulder, right over his scars. "Eban, I've been recovering, so it hasn't felt like smothering." Then he narrowed his deep brown eyes. "However, you have to remember that once I'm well, I *will* require a little more independence."

Moaning softly, Eban nodded. "I'll try."

"We'll get there," Graham assured, his words filling Eban with relief.

"No, I don't mean a tux for your wedding," Kaiser cut in, reminding Eban why they were there. "I mean, there's a charity auction gala at the end of next week. I had originally RSVPed myself and Arthur, but we will make excuses and change the tickets to you and Eban instead." The alpha shrugged as continued, "We'll mention you both taking our place in your wedding announcement."

"So the stalker has a chance to try to plan something there?" Graham mused slowly.

"Exactly," Kaiser replied. "Of course, we'll have plenty of discreet security placed around the space."

Graham raised his hand as if needing to ask a question. At least he didn't wait for permission to speak. "Wait." Graham lowered his hand. "Wouldn't it make more sense to have Beta William and the police captain take your place?"

William chuckled. "We're already signed up to go."

John groaned. "I hate monkey suits."

Leaning over the arms of their chairs, William grabbed John's hand and lifted his palm to his mouth and kissed it. "But you look so damn good in it, baby."

The older man's nostrils flared, and his hazel eyes darkened a little. "Stop it, mate," he warned. "Before I need to turn you over my knee."

William growled softly, his eyes narrowing. "Promises, promises."

Alpha Kaiser rose from his position, tugging Arthur with him. "And on that note, I think we have to get started."

"Wait, Alpha," Ovram cried, lifting his tablet. "We didn't talk about possible suspects, yet."

With an annoyed grumble, Alpha Kaiser lowered back to his seat. He tucked Arthur close to him, then pointed at William. "You, keep a civil tongue in your head. I have no desire to hear about what you get up to with your mate."

Arthur snorted. "How is them talking about spanking any different than you nearly getting me off on the dance floor?"

Alpha Kaiser's cheeks actually pinked just a smidge, something Eban had *never* seen before. "I didn't do it, though, did I? We ended up in the men's room."

"Aaaaand, more than *I* needed to know about *your* sex life, too, bro," William cut in with a laugh, his green eyes dancing with mirth. He clapped his hands and turned his attention to Ovram. "Okay, Ov. Whaddaya got?"

"Well, most in your unit were guys who didn't have family," Ovram began, peering at Graham. "Or very little. The notable exception was Linus, who had a wife and daughter, but they're living in Michigan with her family."

Graham hummed softly, a small smile playing across his lips. "Marilyn is a good woman, and her and Linus's daughter is an absolute gem." He grimaced. "I'm sorry they lost him."

Ovram nodded. "She's doing pretty well, from all the reports I've found." Then he turned back to his tablet and tapped it again. "Brice had a brother, but they were estranged. They hadn't talked in over four years. He's also halfway across the country."

"So, do you have *any* suspects?" Alpha Kaiser cut in.

Nodding again, Ovram held up his hand for patience. "Brendan had a girlfriend and a boyfriend." He glanced up and added, "Neither knew about each other, and both live in Sacramento."

"Damn," Cuzco muttered. "Jerk." Then his eyes widened, and he focused on Graham. "Um, sorry. Didn't mean to call your, uh, brother-in-arms a, well —"

Graham held up a hand, stalling Cuzco's ramblings. "Relax, man. When it came to getting laid and relationships, Brendan was an ass. He had at least two on the hook at any given time, plus he enjoyed bar hook-ups." Graham grimaced and shook his head. "Me and a couple other guys sometimes wondered if we should tell his" — he waved his hand absently — "whatever they were called, but we didn't want to mess with the military bro-code."

"Anyone else?" William asked, crossing his legs at the ankles.

Ovram shrugged. "Afraid not." He focused on Graham. "The guys in your unit really were mostly loners."

Graham nodded. "It's why we were family to each other." He rubbed his chest. "And why it hurt so much to lose them."

"Did you hear back from Mick about possibly getting hate mail, too?"

Eban remembered he'd been the other human Price had been able to rescue. He'd been given a medical discharge, too. Mick had ended up with extensive scarring on his face and right arm, deep enough to impact his muscles, meaning he could no longer fulfill military physical requirements. Although he'd managed to keep all his limbs.

Sure hope he's grateful for that.

Nodding his head at Kaiser's question, Graham admitted, "He said he hasn't seen anything, but if that changes, he'll contact me."

CHAPTER EIGHT

Graham made it down the runway without throwing up.
He figured that was a good sign.

God, I spent days in dark dripping jungles with the threat of massive spiders and snakes attacking at every turn, not to mention enemies, and I'm stressed out by a bunch of photographers and news people? Ugh!

It didn't help that those same news people were hollering questions the entire time Eban helped him from the limo and walked him down the aisle.

Graham suddenly missed his cane. He hadn't needed it for a week, but it would have been nice to wield at a particularly nasty and vulgar reporter. As if he was going to comment on his big man's dick size.

What the fuck is wrong with people? Asking intrusive questions about other people's sex lives. Disgusting!

Focusing on getting through the evening, Graham took the bottle of beer from Eban and did his best to pay attention when William introduced him to . . . whoever they were talking to now.

Shit!

"Do you want to walk through the hall and view the items up for auction?"

While Graham knew Eban asked because it was part of their play to see if his stalker would be around to see him and make a move, Graham actually found himself interested.

"That would be fantastic, Eban."

Eban took his hand and tucked it into the crook of his elbow. "Come on, my love. I heard there's a luxury vacation package to the Bahamas available." He winked. "You know how I love warm ocean waters." Dipping his head, Eban rumbled into his ear. "It'd make an excellent honeymoon destination."

Feeling Eban's warm breath fan over his ear, Graham shivered as his blood heated. Even with his discomfort at the situation that he found himself in, his prick still managed to start to thicken.

"Lead the way, my love," Graham muttered huskily, then grabbed his champagne flute from where he'd left it on their nearby table and downed the rest of it.

Graham set the flute down on a nearby waiter's tray, then snagged a second one. He didn't actually intend to get drunk, and it would take far more than two or three champagne flutes to do the job. Instead, he knew he had to keep up appearances.

If the stalker is around, I want him to think I'm relaxed and vulnerable.

Eban led Graham out of the ballroom and into a massive hall. There were tables set up intermittently along both sides of the wall. Items and pictures were propped up on the tables.

"Let's see what else we can find," Eban stated, drawing him toward the nearest table. "Oh, look at that. Emerald cuff links."

Graham knew Eban feigned interest. Neither of them gave a shit about such things. Still, he hummed in an appreciative way, hoping he pulled off his role.

For the next forty minutes, Graham and Eban moseyed down the hall and looked at the different items up for silent auction. They didn't bother bidding on anything. As far as Graham was concerned—and he could tell Eban didn't care either—art, clothing, jewelry, and most vacation packages weren't of interest to either of them.

Graham did notice Eban pausing a little longer before the Bahama package he'd mentioned.

When dinner was called, Eban guided him back into the dining hall. They found their table and took their chairs next to William and John. Fortunately, the beta of the pod was damn down to earth, and easily made small talk . . . with everyone at the table. He drew people in with amusing tales of what happened at the park and funny anecdotes.

Graham even laughed a few times. He ate his food and managed to chat a little with the others at the table. A couple thanked him for his service, while another pair ignored him completely.

Whatever.

Spotting the time on the clock — the silent auction was just about coming to a close — Graham whispered, "I need to hit the head. I'll be right back."

Eban smirked up at him, playing along. "Need company?"

Shaking his head, Graham gave him a fond smile. "You're incorrigible."

"Only for you, handsome."

Rising from his seat, Graham squeezed his lover's shoulder, then made his way out of the ballroom. According to the schedule, there would be announcements thanking contributors shortly. Then they would tell who'd won what.

Graham hurried to the silent auction table he wanted and took in the half-full silent auction bidding bowl on the table. While he wasn't rich by any means, he wanted to take his man on a trip he would appreciate. After doing a mental calculation in his head, Graham scribbled his information and the amount he would be willing to pay on a ballot slip. He folded it and dropped it into the jar.

"Oh, isn't that nice. Trying to buy your bruiser of a lover a nice vacation. How much did you pay those guys to try to protect you?"

Slowly, Graham straightened and turned. He recognized that voice. Except, he didn't believe it until he stared the man in the eye. "Mick? What are you doing here?"

Curling the left side of his mouth, Mick stared him down. "What do you think I'm doing here, Graham?" he hissed, easing closer. "I told you that you didn't deserve to live, and I've come to make certain that happens."

"But—"

Before Graham could finish his sentence, Mick snapped his left hand up. He stabbed something into his upper arm. The pain of the pinprick was secondary to the icy cold that seeped through his veins. Graham's knees immediately began to buckle.

Mick swiftly wrapped his arm around his waist. Grabbing Graham's near arm, he slung it around his own shoulders. He began urging them toward the side exit.

Graham's mind spun.

Mick is behind the letters?

"Why?"

Oh gods. Do I really sound that slurred?

Sneering, Mick muttered, "Because Price chose you over Brice. Brice should have come back. Not you."

Why would he care more about Brice?

"Hey, can you open that door for me, man?" Mick's cajoling voice made Graham refocus. "My buddy had one glass too many and needs a few seconds of fresh air."

"Here you are, sirs," someone said.

Graham opened his mouth, intending to ask for help. Except, then they were past the man dressed in a hotel uniform. He found himself stumbling across a darkened parking lot toward a vehicle.

Damn. What the fuck did Mick spike me with?

Graham still didn't know before he was shoved into a vehicle's back seat, and his mind sank into unconsciousness.

The first thing Graham became aware of was whistling. The second was the smell of the ocean and the rolling of a boat underneath his cold body. Prying open his eyelids, he realized he'd been stripped to his undershirt and pants. That was too bad, because as much as he'd hated wearing the tux, he knew it must have been damn expensive.

Spotting Mick in his peripheral vision to his right, Graham allowed his eyelids to slide shut. He took a few minutes to test his strength as he assessed the scene with his other senses. His arms were strapped together at his wrists. His legs had been left unbound, which seemed odd to him.

Blood. I smell blood.

After a quick mental inspection of himself, Graham realized the scent didn't come from him. Even though his head still hurt from whatever Mick had pumped into him and his limbs were a bit lethargic, he didn't actually hurt anywhere.

What the hell?

Graham peeled open his eyelids again and slowly panned the area. He was definitely on a boat. Something small, like a fishing boat that stayed close to shore in good weather. He had a chill because his left cheek and body lay against the damp, carpet-like fabric that covered the wood beneath him. Every once in a while, an ocean wave splashed over the hull of the boat and hit his legs.

Turning his head just a smidge, Graham discovered the source of the blood smell. His stomach clenched, and his heart rate picked up.

Well, fuck.

Mick stood at the stern of the boat. Over and over, whistling happily, he dipped a scooper into a twenty-five-gallon bucket. Then he emptied it over the side of the boat.

Chum splashed into the water — bits of meat and plenty of blood.

Oh god.

Deciding the only thing that might help him to delay the

inevitable, being tossed into chum-filled waters, was to wait and stall, Graham lay still.

That didn't work for long . . . or maybe he'd been out for some time and Mick had been emptying the bucket for a while.

"I know you're awake, Graham." Mick straightened and sneered at him. "You have no idea how long I've been waiting and dreaming and planning for this moment."

Then Mick scooped into the bucket again. He poured it over Graham's head, drawing a gasp and cry from him.

Mick laughed, his grinning smile maniacal. "You should have died instead of my Brice. My Brice should have come home with me, just like always." He shook his head. "That damn vampire picked you, though." Mick's eyes narrowed as his smile turned feral. "I'll take care of you, then fix him, too. He won't expect a thing."

"Yes, he will," Graham countered, trying to blink the blood from his eyes. "I emailed him. He'll know when he hears of my death."

Scoffing, Mick shrugged negligently. "I play the saddened military buddy. He'll never suspect it was me."

Before Graham could figure out a counter to Mick's claims—*God, Mick and Brice were lovers? How did I miss that*—Mick grabbed onto Graham's fake leg and heaved.

Graham felt his prosthesis separate from his flesh. The fabric cap attached to his limb tugged painfully at his implant. He felt his flesh tear, and he screamed as pain seared through his freshly-healed stump.

The cold splash of water dashed away the dark spots that were threatening his vision.

Over the roar of the waves and the blood going through his head, Graham just managed to hear Mick yell, "Have a nice snack!"

Then an engine fired.

All Graham could concentrate on was keeping the pain at bay.

"His tracker has stopped," Dare stated.

Eban snarled softly. "Tell me where."

Dare lifted his chin and smirked. "A few miles off Cora's Point."

Grinning ferally, Eban laughed. "Let's go."

Cora's Point was a favorite fishing spot for humans going after large tuna. Occasionally, sharks infested that water, too. Even as excitement at meeting the asshole who'd taken his mate surged through him, there was trepidation as well.

Stripping next to his fellow enforcer, Eban tossed his clothes every which way. He didn't care what happened to them. He wasn't even naked by the time he strode into the water and initiated his shift.

Eban's shark burst from his skin, more than ready to go after their mate. What remained of his clothing fell away from his expanding form. As soon as he could, he swished his tail and started swimming as fast as he could to Cora's Point.

As much as Eban had wanted to leap into the water as soon as they'd spotted the tracker—placed in the waist of Graham's trouser seam—indicate his mate was somewhere on the ocean, he hadn't known which way to go. They'd had to wait. After all, they couldn't use a tracker underwater. Now, however, nothing could keep him from swimming swiftly to Graham's side.

To Eban's pleasure, he nearly instantly noticed Dare's massive octopus form flanking him to the right. He swam quickly, knowing he could get there far faster than any boat. Eban was a damn big shark. Fortunately, since Dare was a giant octopus, his massive form could easily keep up.

Eban noticed the scent of blood, and he rumbled in annoyance. It would make it more difficult to track his own lover's smell with the animal fluid permeating the water. Then Eban spotted smaller sharks slicing through the water ahead, heading toward the source of the blood.

Putting on a burst of speed, Eban snarled to himself. He swished his tail rapidly, biting at the other sharks as he passed them. The splash caught his attention, and he spotted something sinking into the water near the stern of a boat.

The boat engine started.

Surging forward again, Eban spotted the way the right pant leg flapped awkwardly. The scent of his mate hit him next. Rumbling his unhappiness, he snapped at the obviously no longer attached prosthesis. With the false leg still trapped in Graham's trouser pants, Eban used his hold to drag his mate through the water and well away from the boat and other sharks.

Eban counted in his head. He needed his mate away from his enemy, but he needed to get him above the water's surface, too. After ten seconds of powering away from the watercraft, Eban released his mate's leg.

Diving and curling, Eban took in the situation. He spotted his lover's open eyes, bulging cheeks, and . . . his bound hands. Turning slightly, Eban slowed his movements as he drew close and offered his dorsal fin.

To Eban's pleasure, Graham kicked and lunged, looping his bound hands around his top fin. Eban surfaced, relieved to hear his mate take in a deep, harsh gasp. He swam slowly, letting his mate catch his breath.

"Eban? Holy shit! How?"

Shifting and turning, Eban easily caught his mate and tugged them both to the surface once more so they floated on the waves. "Tracking devices in your clothes," Eban told him. "More of Ovram's shit."

Graham nodded, obviously probably understanding more than Eban did about such things.

Graham clung to him, and there was pain twisted on his lips. "What about Mick?"

"He on the boat?" Eban asked, vacantly recalling Mick as one of the saved soldiers on the mission.

When Eban felt Graham nod against his chest, he pointed. "If he's on that boat, he won't be a problem anymore."

His mate sucked in a gasp of surprise. "What the hell?"

"That's Dare," Eban explained as they watched the tentacles of the giant octopus wrap around the small craft and begin destroying it. "He's taking it down. Your attacker is no more."

"Wow."

Eban nuzzled, kissed, and licked Graham's cheek. "Now. I'm going to shift back to my shark, you're going to drape your arms over my fin and straddle my back, and I'm going to take us home." After another kiss, Eban added, "After you get medical attention to your leg, we're going to start our life stress-free. You ready for that?"

Graham clutched him close as he groaned. "Hell, yeah, my shark. There's nothing on this earth I want more."

After a nod and another kiss, Eban shifted back to his great white. He carefully caught Graham's roped hands on his fin, then patiently waited for him to get situated on his back. Finally, with Dare following at his side and Graham hanging onto his back, Eban returned to their home.

Can't wait for that low-stress life to begin . . . with my mate.

ABOUT THE AUTHOR

Charlie started writing fantasy when she was eight, and after stumbling onto her first erotic romance at age nineteen, she realized her true calling. She now focuses on writing gay erotic romance, normally of the paranormal variety, with heroes of all kinds. With the help and support of her husband, Charlie finally fulfilled one of her life-long goals . . . move to acreage with her horses. You can often find her curled up with her laptop and a cup of tea or glass of wine, creating her next adventure. Charlie enjoys exploring the mountains of her new Oregon home on horseback, 4-wheeler, or motorcycle.

She can be reached at ch.richards2010@yahoo.com
Or visit her at www.charlie-richards.com

www.ingramcontent.com/pod-product-compliance
Lightning Source LLC
Chambersburg PA
CBHW070538130626
46555CB00003B/1475